"The whole world is divided...into two parts: one is she, and there is all happiness, hope, light; the other is where she is not, and there is dejection and darkness."

Leo Tolstoy - War and Peace

"Man holds the remedy in his own hands, and lets everything go its own way, simply through cowardice... I should like to know what people fear worst: whatever is contrary to their usual habits, I imagine."

Fyodor Dostoevsky - Crime and Punishment

"There is a stubbornness about me that never can bear to be frightened at the will of others. My courage always rises at every attempt to intimidate me."

Jane Austen - Pride and Prejudice

"I am no bird; and no net ensnares me; I am a free human being with an independent will."

Charlotte Brontë - Jane Eyre

18 YEARS IN LOCKDOWN

Sannan Rymer

CONTENTS

1 THE CITY **1**
- 1 JAGO'S CHILDHOOD **2**
- 2 VISITATION DAY **4**
- 3 THE SAFETY GUARD **7**
- 4 CARE HOUSE **11**
- 5 STRANGER ON THE TRAIN **16**
- 6 DEATH IN THE FAMILY **20**

2 THE WRITERS **23**
- 1 FIRE ALARM **24**
- 2 RUMER RECEIVES A LETTER **28**
- 3 THE OTHERS **33**
- 4 THOUGHTS OF ESCAPE **40**
- 5 PLANS OF ESCAPE **43**
- 6 UNDERGROUND **48**
- 7 CONVERSATIONS IN THE DARK **54**
- 8 DAYLIGHT AND THE RIVER **61**

3 AMICA **67**
- 1 JAGO RECEIVES A MESSAGE **68**
- 2 JAGO'S DECISION **75**
- 3 A SECRET PLAN **77**
- 4 ESCAPE FROM THE CITY **80**
- 5 THE PERIMETER **86**
- 6 INTRODUCTIONS **88**
- 7 WATER AND FIRE **93**
- 8 ENCOUNTER ON THE FARM **98**

4 FIRST CHILD **100**
    1 ENDURING THE WINTER **101**
    2 DRONE **106**
    3 AMICA TALKS TO JAGO **111**
    4 HYA SHARES WITH THE WRITERS **114**

5 BOOKS **117**
    1 RETURN TO THE UNDERGROUND **118**
    2 CHURCH SPIRE **122**
    3 THE NEW FAMILY **127**
    4 BODHI **132**
    5 LOOKING AFTER FREYA AND FOX **141**
    6 CLEO HAS A CHILD **148**
    7 DRAVEN READS 18 YEARS IN LOCKDOWN **152**
    8 DRAVEN RETURNS TO THE VILLAGE **158**

6 THE VILLAGE **169**
    1 ENGAGEMENT **170**
    2 THE PRAIRIES BY THE VILLAGE **174**
    3 THE WEDDING **179**
    4 MAXEN GOES TO THE QUARRY **184**
    5 AMICA'S REGRET **192**

7 PASSENGERS **197**
    1 THE RANGERS **198**
    2 WAITING IN THE PARK **202**
    3 BOARDING THE TRAIN **206**
    4 RETURN JOURNEY **213**
    5 COMING HOME **219**
    6 A VISITOR FROM THE CITY **226**
    7 BY THE FIRE **234**

1
THE CITY

1
JAGO'S CHILDHOOD

He had been relocated when he was just a child. Save a few idyllic memories, he had barely any recollection of his life prior. He had been moved, like the others, from the outside and into the city. To accommodate him and the new arrivals, all available housing in the city was divided up into smaller apartments, called units, and each outsider was assigned one.

So Jago's unit was small: comprised of only a bed, a bathroom, and an integrated kitchen. He only had enough room in the space around his bed to place one chair. This chair, he'd turned outwards from the rest of the room so it faced the only window. In the early evening, the cracks in the boards covering the window would allow just enough light through for patterns to emerge in the window pane. So as the sun fell, he would sit in his chair and watch the light glinting in the glass, it seeming to appear differently each time.

As he watched, Jago would think back to his childhood, as he usually did; for the light reminded him of the sunshine outdoors. As the daylight began to fade, he would close his eyes, and try to remember his life before the city.

There was one memory he would often picture. In it, he was a child, acting like a child, and thinking in light childish ways. There were fields. There were other kids. There was a football being kicked about. Then Jago remembered falling, falling in the field and grazing his knee. From the corner of his eye he could see the other kids trying to withhold their laughter, waiting to see if he was okay. He could feel — even now in his chair — as he lay on the grass clutching his knee, the fresh air drying his moist cheeks and sweated brow, and his eyes squinting against the hot sun. But soon, he was back to his feet again, chasing the ball, as if nothing had happened.

Later that day, in that same memory, the sun had now fallen and Jago was in his childhood bed. He remembered looking out at the stars and feeling the draft from his ajar bedroom window. He had a crumpled book in his hand and could feel his heavy eyes slowly shutting as he read. When he could no longer see them on the page, he would invent the words from his book instead. Finally, he heard the wish of sweet dreams from his mother, and Jago would fall to sleep.

But then, his childhood bedroom turned to black. He opened his eyes and he was back in the city, back in his chair, the darkness all around him, the light from the window now passed. He closed his eyes again and tried and willed to go back to the places in his memories; back to the fields and back to his childhood home. But no matter how hard he tried to get back there, he could not. Jago was alone again.

2
VISITATION DAY

He woke, hearing his food delivery placed noisily outside his door — a neighbour must have let them in again. Jago was hazy. He'd slept sitting on his chair in front of the window, as he sometimes would, and had been dreaming. He couldn't ever remember much from his dreams, only vague visions; a fog of memories and imagination; he was never sure which was which, but whatever emotion he felt was left to linger long after.

Somewhere in there, were memories from his childhood, as they often were. But last night, they had contorted and become something else. Some other unwelcome force had taken his memories and twisted them into a nightmare, and Jago had woken, uneasy what he had seen was his reality.

He tried to widen his eyes and shake loose these feelings. He looked around his room, hoping the familiar shapes would realign his skewed thoughts, and he looked up at the window, where the light might restart him. But he remained dazed, and at odds.

He wanted to stay in his chair but today he couldn't.

He stirred, lifted himself up and laboured to the sink, filling his water bottle routinely and sipping from it. He thought of his arduous journey ahead and resented having to go each year. Everyone else could talk on the social, but not her, she had insisted; they *had* to meet in person.

Jago had recalled their early attempts to talk online. His mother had detested it immediately, finding it impersonal, and hassling. She was averse to technology, old fashioned like that, too stubborn to conform. So when she'd been re-homed to the outskirts just days from her seventieth birthday, Jago had applied for visitation to her. Arguing on the flimsy grounds she was unable to use the social in her condition, his yearly pass was granted. She would see him on the same day every year, and today was that day.

Jago glanced at his phone, left on the kitchen worktop from the previous night. His journey for the day was programmed into it. A car would take him from his building to the district station. There, he would board a train to the outskirts station. A second car would then take him to the care house where his mother was kept.

He put his water bottle down and went to collect his food box still waiting outside. He unpacked it, keeping one ration out for his breakfast. As he ate, his phone buzzed. He checked it: the car would soon be arriving, the countdown for it appearing on his screen.

One hundred, ninety nine, ninety eight, ninety seven...

Jago downed the last of his food, then dressed hurriedly: he couldn't miss the car, there was no replacement. If he missed it, she would have to wait another year.

Seventy nine, seventy eight, seventy seven...

He grabbed his phone and left, his unit door closing behind him.

Sixty two, sixty one, sixty, fifty nine...

He came down two flights of stairs to the lobby and rushed outside. The light blinded him, but he allowed his eyes no time to adjust, running to the waiting car's open door and getting in. He hadn't dared look around.

Thirty two, thirty one, thirty, twenty nine, twenty eight...

As he shuffled across the back seat, the door swung shut abruptly behind. Though he still always looked from habit, the car windows were boarded over, just like in his room. He couldn't see a thing through them.

He turned back to the interior, where he saw the same sign again in front of him. It was always there; fitted to the blacked out divide between the passenger seat and the front compartment. It was just illuminated enough by the stray daylight filtering through for him to read it. But Jago didn't bother; he'd seen it so many times before, he already knew what it said.

STAY SAFE, STAY INSIDE.
SAVE OUR CITY.

Three, Two, one, zero.

The car started, rocking Jago forward. He sat back but the rigid frame of the seat, stripped of its padding, pressed awkwardly into his back. He adjusted for a slight reprieve then lay his head as comfortably he could over the lip of the seat. He closed his eyes, tried to steady his anxiously beating heart and entreated a safe journey.

3
THE SAFETY GUARD

The car arrived into the district station, the door opened. Jago alighted and approached the security gate at the entrance. Then he saw it. His core lurched uncontrollably and instinctively. It was unmoving, and even more disturbing because of it. Its consuming figure; broad as it was tall, was dressed in dark uniform and fully decked in armour. In large white letters, the word SAFETY was stencilled across its breast plate, the words, KEEPING YOU SAFE just below. Not an inch of skin could be seen on it; its face was masked, its eyes tinted behind a visor, a helmet covered its head, and ridged gloves its hands. In one of those hands, it held a large perspex shield, while the other hovered over a baton holstered to its side.

Jago hurried to the gate, keeping his eye firmly away from the guard. He scanned his phone, ready in his hand, over the security panel. The blue light turned green and it opened.

He passed through to the main terminal: a large hanger with a row of platforms aligned perpendicularly to the entrance. The scope of it was always arresting and he allowed himself just a brief moment to appreciate the open space.

He continued to the platform, coming to the final security barrier just before it. Another guard was patrolling. He scanned his phone, still in his hand, over the panel as before. This time, the blue light did not turn green, but turned red.

Jago sensed the immediate attention of the guard. Still, he didn't dare look. He tried again, scanning his phone, more pronouncedly a second time. But the red light stayed red. His heart was pounding. He scanned again, then a fourth time, then a fifth time. He could hear heavy footsteps behind him. He scanned again; at last: a green light. The gate opened. He rushed through. He did not look back.

He came out from behind the barrier. The train was waiting at the platform. It filled his view. It shimmered like air in the heat. A pocket of light streamed down from the shutters above and ran a sheen across its roof, beads of condensation, lit up, trickled down its side. The train was perspiring, it was impatient to leave.

Then, Jago's eye was caught by movement up ahead. There was another guard. And in its hand it had gripped the collar of a civilian. They jostled for a moment further along the platform. The guard then shoved him onto the train. He toppled backwards, falling awkwardly to the floor. The guard's mask undulated, then its voice carried down the platform to him.

'This one, I said!'

The train doors slid closed over the feet of the floored passenger.

Then a much more imminent voice startled Jago.

'You! Get in!' it said.

Jago's heart convulsed again. He tried to muster a response but the voice shouted again first.

'Now! Move!'

He obeyed and scurried through the open door of the nearest carriage. He glimpsed behind him as the doors closed and saw the guard walking away. The doors touched and he breathed a sigh of relief, his heartbeat slowing. He couldn't see the guard any more, or the platform: the train windows were boarded over, just like everything else.

He turned. The carriage was empty, as it usually was. He looked for a seat on the rows either side of the interior, but all were torn, stained or broken. Jago compromised on one and sat down. In front of him were the signs again, which lined the walls above the seats opposite.

STAY SAFE, STAY INSIDE.
SAVE OUR CITY.

DO YOU HAVE YOUR TRAVEL PASS TODAY?
NO PASS, NO TRAVEL.
OFFENDERS WILL BE DOCKED.

ARE YOU DOING YOUR BIT TO HELP OUR CITY?
ONLY TOGETHER WE CAN.

IF YOU SEE ANYTHING SUSPICIOUS, OR ANYONE ACTING SUSPICIOUSLY,
PLEASE REPORT IT IMMEDIATELY TO YOUR SAFETY TEAM.
THANK YOU.

The signs continued along the carriage wall until Jago couldn't make them out.

The train started slowly into motion. The carriage lights dimmed and it left the station. Jago sat back, closing his eyes again. But then the announcements played over the loudspeaker, jolting him to. The voice was upbeat and amiable.

'TO HELP ENSURE THAT EVERYONE ON BOARD FEELS SAFE THROUGHOUT THE JOURNEY, PLEASE REMAIN SEATED AT ALL TIMES. REMEMBER, NO FOOD OR DRINK IS TO BE CONSUMED ON BOARD. AND PLEASE ENSURE A MINIMUM OF TEN SEATS BETWEEN YOU AND ANY OTHER PASSENGERS. YOUR MOBILE PHONE AND TRAVEL PASS MUST BE KEPT WITH YOU FOR THE ENTIRE JOURNEY AND BE READY FOR INSPECTION AT ALL TIMES. ANYONE FOUND WITHOUT THEIR CREDENTIALS *WILL* BE DOCKED. IF YOU SEE ANYONE NOT ADHERING TO THESE RULES, PLEASE REPORT THEM IMMEDIATELY TO YOUR SAFETY TEAM. THIS WILL HELP ENSURE YOUR OWN SAFETY AND THE SAFETY OF EVERYONE ON BOARD. SAFETY IS OUR NUMBER ONE PRIORITY.'

The train arrived into the outskirts station.

The lights lifted and the carriage doors opened. Jago left the train, checking the platform; there were no guards this time. He glanced at his phone, the countdown for the next car had already started.

Fifty four, fifty three, fifty two, fifty one...

He hurried to the platform barrier, scanning his phone over the panel, then came out into the main terminal, this one far smaller than the last. Still, there were no guards; Jago remembered there often weren't out here.

Twenty five, twenty four...

He passed through the exit to the outside, noticing for the first time the warm spring day around him. He put his hand out against the blinding light and could make out the outline of the car. He went over to it, got in and checked his phone.

Four, three, two, one, zero.

The car left the station.

4
CARE HOUSE

The outskirts had been left to spoil over time. Once the industrial hub of the city, it was now in ruins; a near wasteland. The car disappeared off tidily behind Jago, so quietly he barely noticed. He was left standing, surrounded by abandoned buildings, all in varying levels of disrepute. Everything was so still here, even quieter than the inner city, and there were hardly ever any guards patrolling this way. The outskirts had only one function now, to house the older population of the city: the most vulnerable. The buildings that were still usable had been reconstituted to house them. They called them care houses.

His mother's building was in front of him. It was a converted warehouse; an ageing brick structure, discoloured and dilapidated. The vast window panels on the front were all now boarded over. But unlike the inner city, as these were rarely surveilled, *these* boards were caked in graffiti, only a few slithers of boarding still left visible underneath. Jago had seen most of it before, but this time, he noticed something new, writing much larger, sprayed expansively over the rest. It caused him to pause.

> Fear Controls.
> Lies Trap.
> Risk Frees.

He kept re-reading it, each time it feeling more aphoristic. He tried to shake it from his head and walk on to the entrance gate, but the words seemed to stay looming overhead.

He scanned his phone over the front panel, another blue light went green and the gate opened. He went inside. A second door opened from the main entrance hallway and Jago passed through it into the visitors' room.

It was long and narrow, with a walkway to the right and then a series of partitions, at right angles to the wall, on the left. The entire left wall was one large transparent screen. All of the partitions had red lights above them, except one, which was blue.

Jago went towards it and entered the bay between the two partitions. A stool was placed there in front of the screen. He sat down, scanned his phone again on the console in front. The blue light on the partition turned green and he could hear another door opening out of sight. He heard the comforting sound of a wheelchair turning. It was his mother's chair. It grew louder. Then she came into view into the dimly lit space on the other side of the screen. She stopped and looked at him. And he looked back.

Each year, she looked older, he thought, and less like his mother. But she had the same complexion and the same warm eyes, which would still radiate when she saw him.

The countdown appeared on the screen between them.

One hundred, ninety nine, ninety eight...

'Hi mum,' Jago said.

'Hello son,' his mother responded.

'There seems to be less and less visitors each year...,' Jago commented.

'Well, most of us are dead, son. So it would be a bit of a wasted trip for them, wouldn't you say?'

Jago smirked, always partial to his mother's mordant humour.

'At least they'd get out of the house,' he retorted.

She half smiled.

'Do they not treat you well then?' Jago added more seriously.

'Yes, they treat us fine,' she replied, 'maybe even better than you lot. At least we get to see a carer once in a while, you don't get to see anyone.'

'For good reason,' Jago responded quickly. He looked down momentarily, then up again. 'So why are people dying then?'

'Just no point in living, is there,' she answered without hesitation, as if prepared, 'Well, why would we all hang on exactly? For the awful food they give us? To be stuck alone in our rooms, only ever seeing the inside of four walls? To be told when we can see our own family? To then wait around till that one day comes?' She snorted derisively. 'No son, most of us would rather get on with it and die.'

She paused, her face still as she thought.

'You know, it's okay for us oldies, at least we'll all be gone soon. You have to live with all of this.'

'Yes, but it's necessary,' Jago responded, promptly again, 'we all have to do our bit.'

Her demeanour changed.

'Really, Jago? Your bit? *Your* bit? What's *your bit* exactly?' she exclaimed, sounding incredulous, 'Is it never leaving your room? Is it never doing an honest day's work ever again? Is it never meeting another human being for the rest of your life? Is that *your* bit?' She tutted.

Seventy two, seventy one, seventy...

'That's not true,' Jago started, 'we can meet people—'

'Online!' she interrupted sharply, 'Online, yes. But that's not the same, is it, not the same at all. But what do I know? You lot can't even tell the difference any more between what's on your screens and what's real life!'

Fifty seven, fifty six, fifty five...

Her last few words lingered. Jago could hear her dismay and the exasperation in her voice; she couldn't fathom the world that he lived in.

'But it's to keep everyone safe,' he implored, 'Honestly, mum, it's not that bad; I have a roof over my head, water, food, a phone...'

He trailed off, he couldn't think of anything else to add. His mother stayed quiet deliberately to emphasise this to him.

'Yes, son, those things are fine,' she said finally, 'but you can't smell the fresh air, can you? You can't watch the sunset, you can't hug someone, or even shake hands. I don't call that living, Jago, that's just existing.'

Twenty six, twenty five, twenty four...

'And you'll never be able to start a family either. Did you even think about that?'

Jago *had* thought about this, he always thought about all of her chiding.

'But I can't do anything about it,' he contested, 'You want me corrected, or killed out there on the streets? The rules are for our own good, they're for our safety, our protection. I can't just think about myself, I have to think about others too.'

His mother leaned in.

'Well, maybe it's time you *did* do something about it, son,' she spoke softly, as though she were telling him a secret, 'We're not supposed to live like this. And *you're definitely* not supposed to live like this.'

Jago was conflicted between her words and his duty to his city. He didn't want to admit there was a part of him that agreed with her.

'It's...,' he stuttered, '...it's only for a little longer. They said it will all be over soon. Then we can go back to normal.'

'Right, just a little longer,' she said sardonically, 'They said that eighteen years ago, Jago. It's never going to end, when will you see that?'

She slowly sat back upright, adding more light-heartedly, 'And don't use me as an excuse. I won't be around forever. I'll be fine without you, don't you worry.'

Jago sighed and looked back at her.

'Guess I'll go get myself thrown in jail then,' he joked, 'From one cell to another.'

She smiled again at his sarcasm.

Sixteen, fifteen, fourteen...

'I think we're running out of time,' she said concluding, 'Just think about what I said, son, please, and don't wallow when I'm gone, I'll be much happier up there, no doubt about it.'

Jago nodded and smiled back.

Ten, nine, eight...

'See you next year, mum,' he said, 'And don't be too mean to those carers, will you, life must be hard enough for them as it is.'

'Would I?' she forbode.

Jago saw her eyes beam at him once more.

'Bye, Jago,' she said.

'Yep, see you.'

Two, one, zero.

Her side of the room went dark. Jago could no longer see her or hear anything from behind the screen. The green light on the partition had turned red and the door he had come through reopened. He stood up quickly, trying not to break emotionally, and he rushed from the room.

He was struck again by the light as he came outside. His eyes adjusted and the shape of the car came into view once more. He got in, sat back calmly, trying to subdue the anguish that was seizing him. But all he could think about was her all alone again, and waiting.

Until next year, mum, he said to himself.

5
STRANGER ON THE TRAIN

'...AND PLEASE ENSURE A MINIMUM OF TEN SEATS BETWEEN YOU AND ANY OTHER PASSENGERS. YOUR MOBILE PHONE AND TRAVEL PASS MUST BE KEPT WITH YOU FOR THE ENTIRE JOURNEY AND BE READY FOR INSPECTION AT ALL TIMES. ANYONE FOUND WITHOUT THEIR CREDENTIALS *WILL* BE DOCKED. IF YOU SEE ANYONE NOT ADHERRING TO THE RULES, PLEASE REPORT THEM IMMEDIATELY TO YOUR SAFETY TEAM. THIS WILL HELP ENSURE YOUR OWN SAFETY AND THE SAFETY OF EVERYONE ON BOARD. SAFETY IS OUR NUMBER ONE PRIORITY.'

Jago was agitated. As he sat on the train, he was no longer feeling sympathy for her, but was obsessing over what his mother had said. She was right, this *was* no way to live. Speaking to her was always to face his own ill content and to confront his own passivity. He had been confined to his room where all he did was resent what had become of his life. Year after year, his suspicions grew as to what was really compelling him to stay there, but still, he never acted. He cursed his own lack of conviction.

Jago was distracted from his thoughts by the sound of footsteps approaching along the platform. They came right up alongside the carriage. Then the door opened and the footsteps entered. Jago daren't look in case they belonged to a guard, his eyes staying rooted to the floor. The footsteps came closer and closer, the light softening around him as the figure approached. Then in his eye line, a pair of trainers came into view; they were blue, and very garish. Guards don't wear trainers, Jago thought, and he was relieved. Then, he noticed one of the trainers had an untied shoe lace and as the other foot took another step, it arched precariously near it. Jago looked up instinctively, concerned this person might trip. But without another step, she sat down on the seats opposite him, carefully placing a bag down next to her.

Jago's eyes shot away again to the floor.

The train continued and Jago was unsettled by her being there: she was too close, he thought, within the ten seat minimum. Why had she sat there when the rest of the carriage was free, it was a clear breach of train rules!

He should message the safety team.

But she might see him doing it.

He would report her at the next station instead.

He tried to look over without being noticed and he eyed the blue trainers again. He thought how incongruous they were against the dull interior of the train. Who would wear such things, he asked himself. Then his curiosity finally bettered him. He turned and looked at the stranger.

This time she wasn't occupied with the seat, or her bag, but met his look with her own. Suddenly, unexpectedly, they found their eyes were locked together, neither of them seeming willing to look away. Jago fought to maintain a stoic countenance but his nervous body was trying to betray him. As they continued to look at each other, Jago began to wonder if the moments passed had been too few to be significant or too many not to be.

Where others would quicken to avoid the guards, he had wandered. He seemed unhurried and languid and marked a withdrawn figure, dislocated from his surroundings. He was a curiosity to her now and she was enmired, intrigued to know more of him.

She had boarded the train as she did every day, but this time, on the same carriage he had. She approached him but he wasn't looking. Then he had glanced over as she sat down, but only fleetingly. She studied him as he stared down at the floor. He seemed troubled now. Was it because of her?

Then his eyes did turn to her and in the dim light, the whites of them stood out. They were dull eyes, sullen and blank. She had seen those eyes many times before: two windows to despondency and lifelessness. But could she see something else in his, buried deeper perhaps? She saw pain, turmoil, perhaps contradiction. Was she just reaching? Or projecting?

His eyes had still not diverted from hers, no flicker of fragility ran across them. She hadn't seen this resoluteness before. But it wasn't confidence, or brashness either, he was hurting, and he was crying out from within that empty shell.

A sound of screeching metal ripped through the carriage. Jago winced. His head spun to the sound. The large internal door had slid open and through it, entered the towering figure of a guard. It approached, the bottom of its shield scraping along each seat as it moved towards them. Larger and larger it came, imposing itself and further darkening the carriage.

It stopped in front of Jago. He was looking away but could feel its presence bearing over him. Its helmet tilted down towards him. Jago's tentative eyes scrolled upwards until he saw the lifeless mask looking back at him. He cowered back into his seat.

'Pass?' it commanded, its orotund voice booming through its mask.

Jago was stupefied, his faculties had deserted him. He froze.

'Pass, now!' it repeated, more intemperately.

Jago tried desperately to speak but found he had no voice.

'Yes, it's-it's-' he stammered, trying to force any words out.

The guard leant in, its face right up to Jago's.

'Pass, civi, it's not difficult.'

Jago reached down to his pocket. His hand was shaking. He tried to pull his phone out but it caught on the inner lining of his trousers. He scrambled trying to free it. As he looked down, he glimpsed the stranger still sitting opposite. She was watching.

Jago paused and his hand seemed to steady. Some bravado had possessed him; he'd realised he could no longer abide anyone seeing him like that: so craven. He rose to his feet. He looked up into the tinted voids of the guard's mask.

'Excuse me!' he said inadvisably, 'We were having a moment there.'

There was a stifled laugh from the seats opposite and Jago unthinkingly glanced over, taking his attention off the guard. This was an error.

He could not compute the pain at first, only his body knew how to respond and he collapsed to the floor. He remembered seeing blood run down between his eyes and nose. Soon his whole face was wet with blood. He felt his top grabbed and he was dragged along the floor to the end of the carriage. He remembered pulses of dull light from the ceiling. And he felt another blow to his ribs. Then another.

With whatever awareness he still had, he looked back at the stranger. She was much smaller now. But even in his blurriness, he thought he could see her still looking back at him. He questioned if his eyes were lying.

Her face was the last thing he remembered.

6
DEATH IN THE FAMILY

Jago was disturbed awake by the brightening of the carriage lights. He felt groggy. The train door near him was open and he felt the cool air from the platform wash over him. He struggled up, managing to lift his torso to a slouched position. There was no sign of anyone in the train car. He noticed the blood on his top and began to recall what had happened. He clutched the side of his head and saw the red on his hands. Using the inside of his top, he tried to wipe as much of it away as he could from his face. He came forward onto his knees, then pulled himself up to his feet and staggered from the carriage.

Checking the platform, Jago saw a guard at the far end. Its back was turned. Seizing the opportunity, he dashed to the security barrier, scanned his phone and passed through. Aware of the blood stains still on him, he walked through the station as fast as he thought wouldn't draw any suspicion. He scanned through the entrance gate and came outside.

The car was there; waiting, willing, and seemingly oblivious. He rushed over and climbed in gratefully. His heart was thumping.

The car left the station, he hadn't bothered checking the countdown this time.

Everything seemed accelerated; the doors of the car, the sign, the blacked out divide, all throbbed. Jago tried to compose himself but he couldn't, the adrenaline was coursing through him. He looked at the blood still on his hands and stared at it. They didn't look like his hands.

The car arrived back at his building. Jago got out and went inside. As he reached the stairwell, the drug of the encounter that had maintained him, suddenly wore off. He felt the pain like another blow as a tide of weariness overwhelmed him. He nearly fell to the ground, only the banister rescuing him. He dragged himself sluggishly up to his room. He opened the door and went straight to his chair and collapsed into it, the door closing behind him. All the dry and rough blood still clung to him, he could feel it like dirt on his skin, but he didn't care.

It was early evening now and the light was starting to fade. His eyes, half closed, looked up at the window again. The glint in the glass as the sun fell sparkled as always. But this time, as he stared at it, he saw the train and the blue trainers and the dead eyes of the guard and the dripping of his own blood, each of them battling for monopoly of his thoughts.

He felt himself falling asleep, he was exhausted. He managed to drop from the chair and drag himself to the refuge of his bed. Within moments of lying down, and for the first time since he was moved to the city, he succumbed to a peaceful, long and dreamless sleep.

Some time had passed since the events on the train. Now the sapping heat of the summer was managing to filter through to even Jago's insulated room. He woke, perspiring, a damp behind his head on the pillow.

His phone was going off.

He turned over to the end of his bed and picked it up from the side table. He was expecting a notification of his docking for the incident on the train, but it wasn't that. It was a message from the care house where his mother stayed. He opened it, read it: his mother had died.

Jago went numb, completely unfeeling. He hardly afforded the message any seriousness at first, what it pronounced seeming so unthinkable. But after a while, the realisation of what had happened overcame him. Now he could think of nothing else.

He became incapacitated by the loss; a great foundation had been torn from under him. He felt paralysed in the purgatory of the unresolved discord with her and racked with the agony of his guilt. He had decried that simple journey to her each year, placing *his* convenience above *her* sensibilities. But worst of all, he had never fulfilled her most basic wish: all she'd wanted was to see him happy, but he hadn't even been able to give her that. She had told him, implored him to stand up and do something, but he never did. He wallowed and pitied himself, and never acted. He had sat in his room and hid and kowtowed, whilst his mother had grown old, haggard and died. Now when Jago remembered his mother, he no longer saw her from his childhood memories; the warm and sweet lady who looked after him. Now he only saw his dying mother; the old, obstinate, carping woman who sat in the sharpness of that limited spotlight, behind that screen.

The regret of inaction and his dereliction of filial duties entombed Jago in his bed. He no longer ate and he barely drank. He became emaciated and pallor, his strength ebbed away. Jago was starting to lose himself and soon he would fade away to nothing.

2
THE WRITERS

1
FIRE ALARM

The huddled bodies shivered in the cold autumnal night. The shrieking alarm was so penetrating, they felt it might never stop ringing. There were ten of them outside the building; the tenantry, waiting to go back into the warmth of the inside. Surrounding them, a team of guards stood and oversaw them. They had formed a barrier of ready shields, enforced by drawn batons raised threateningly. The group watched them nervously.

Hyacinth stood as one of the ten occupants. She felt exhilarated. She could feel the others hemmed in around her. She hardly remembered the last time she was this close to anyone else. The clothes of the person nearest brushed up against her and Hya was sure she could sense the tenseness in her; the accelerated breathing, her head twitching agitatedly around. It was unlike anything in Hya's unsympathetic and inanimate room.

She shouted over the alarm to her.

'What's your name?'

The addressed turned her head to Hya. Her eyes were wide with fright. They darted from Hya to the guards, then back again. Then to Hya's surprise, she leant towards her, lifting her sleeve up to cover her moving lips, and answered.

'Er, Rumer,' she said fragilely.

'What?' said Hya; the alarm was deafening, she couldn't hear a thing.

'Mm...,' came a hesitant response, but then she took a deep breath, and shouted back, 'Rumer!'

Rumer heard herself and realised how loud she'd been. She recoiled, looking in horror towards the guards again, praying her voice hadn't carried.

'No talking!' one of them ordered. It moved closer to them.

The group compacted together.

Hya was fascinated by their reaction. The two at the front of the group had raised their arms out either side, as if to shield the ones behind. Despite none of them having ever met, they still had an instinct to protect each other.

The guard came up to Rumer. Hya stepped into its path.

'One more word…,' it threatened, pointing over Hya's shoulder at Rumer, who averted her eyes to the ground.

Hya stood between them unflinchingly. She held her face, pugnacious, right up to the guard as it inspected her.

'When can we go back in?' someone else shouted, taking away the guard's attention.

A few of the others followed suit.

'Yes, we've been out here for ages.'

'You can't just keep us outside forever.'

'There's clearly no fire. Let us go back in.'

Hya was impressed, the group were starting to stand up for themselves.

The guard moved towards the one who'd spoke first. It went right up to him and shoved him back with both hands. 'No questions!' it shouted. The force toppled him but he didn't fall, the others had caught him.

They were beginning to support each other, thought Hya. They were signalling their solidarity and cohesion to the guards. And it worked, they advanced no further. Both sides remained poised for further incitement.

The standstill was interrupted by the plangent rumbling of a fire truck. It pulled up alongside the building. Several figures jumped out of the vehicle and ran inside.

'Finally,' came the first voice again sarcastically, the same one who had been shoved.

At this, the guard's patience ran out. It struck out at him with its baton. He was able to raise a defensive arm but was struck hard on the elbow. He cried out. Then his head snapped back to the guard with enraged eyes. The others put their arms out in front of him and this seemed to pacify him enough.

'Hey, leave him alone!' one of them shouted.

A second guard then entered the fray, gunning for *this* person. It swung at her. She turned away to avoid the blow but the baton tore across her back. She fell to her knees, arching forward in pain. She caught the eye of the other who'd been struck and they shared a consolidating glance. The rest of the group then moved in front of both of them, shielding them.

Hya could see the animus building. The group were bellicose and at the next provocation, they would surely retaliate.

But then the alarm stopped, and somehow this punctured the tension. Hya felt her ears pulsate as they tried to hear something that was no longer there. The figures ran back out of the building and came up to the guards.

'It's been contained,' one of them reported, '...Started in one of the rooms, probably just burnt rations, nothing major. You can take them back inside now.'

They turned from them and filtered back into the truck and left.

'Waste of time,' one of the guards huffed disapprovingly.

'Get them back inside,' another one ordered.

The guards reformed and encircled the group again. With the sly and constant agitation of the alarm sound now gone, the group were much more biddable. Most of their thoughts had turned to the warmth of their rooms and shelter from the cold. They were compliant enough now to be funnelled back into the building without further incident. Each was ensured they returned to their correct unit, then the guards made a final sweep. They checked the windows and doorways were boarded over and all the signs were still in place. Content, they quitted the building and returned to their cars. They departed the scene and the street was left with the events of that evening its secret.

Later that night, Hya was laying on her bed and unable to sleep. She was picturing all the faces she'd seen outside. Then she placed them each in their rooms. She imagined what they might be doing and wondered what they might be thinking. They would all be alone together again, just as they were before.

Rumer, that was her name; Hya remembered her most of all, the only name she had to put to one of those faces. She saw her frightened face looking back at her again and she felt sorry for her. But then she heard that bold and forthright shout of hers too.

She pictured the ones who had protected the others and the ones who had stood their ground. They had all seemed so strong together. But now they were divided. They were under the same roof, with nothing but a few thin walls between them, yet somehow they still seemed so distant.

Hya wished for them to be together again. She wanted that same feeling, outside in the cold, as the disaffected. She wanted to be amongst them again, part of them, she yearned for that excitement.

She wanted the group to be strong again.

2
RUMER RECEIVES A LETTER

The following morning Rumer woke after a disrupted night of sleep. The artefact of the ringing in her ears hadn't let the events of the prior evening seem any less intense. She could still see the faceless guards and feel the trapped bodies huddled against her in the cold. For just a moment, she thought she was still outside and the hairs on her skin pricked up; a sensation she couldn't remember last having. Then the face of that woman decidedly entered her mind, the one who had asked her name. She had seemed so oddly calm during it all.

Rumer stretched out, her feet and hands reaching to the ends of her bed. She looked at the slithers of light between the cracks in the boarded up window of her unit. The light decided her not to go back to sleep. She swung her legs outside the frame of the bed and onto the floor. With a sigh, she rose and uncurled her back, stretching her arms out again. She wandered over to her kitchenette to see what food she had, opened the fridge drawer and took out a ration. She opened it. The green mush always made her long for old food. It was supposed to provide all the nutrients the body needed, is what they said, but this didn't make it taste any better. She pined for anything else, any food at all from before the changes. The memory alone of old food: snacks, chocolate and meals served on plates, was enough to make her mind salivate.

As she put down the ration, she noticed a flash of white from the other side of her room. It hadn't been there previously. She checked what she thought she saw. There, on her otherwise bare floor, was a piece of white paper, just inside the door.

Her insides churned and her body flushed: contraband, in her room! She resolved at once to leave it, never touch it and forever walk around it. In time, it might just sink or vanish into the floor. Surely she couldn't be in trouble if she just ignored it.

A day passed and the piece of paper remained untouched by Rumer. But an unquenchable curiosity grew as she became captivated by the machiavelli of it all. She glanced at the boarded up windows in case somehow, someone could be watching her and she tip-toed tentatively over to the paper. She sat down next to it, covered her hand with her sleeve and with a tremulous arm, lifted the folded paper up to check it. A small pen fell and rolled out. It seemed to roll forever across her floor, sounding like thunder to her. Now there were two banned items in her possession! Panic gripped her again, she shot a glance to her window and to her door. Then she took a deep breath and tried to calm herself, she reminded herself there was nothing in her room but her, the paper and the pen.

She pulled over the fold of the note. There was handwriting on the inside, something she hadn't seen since she was a child. It transported her back momentarily. She looked over the paper; every mark on it was unique; the lines, the curls, the dots, the crosses, there were even smudges which interested her. The pressure of the pen was constantly changing, the leading was never straight and no letters were ever the same twice. She found the imperfections compelling.

Rumer lay the paper down on the floor and flattened it out to read. Her excitement was only rivalled by her anxiety.

Rumer,

I know I'm taking a risk in writing to you, but for some reason, I want to trust you. You could tell them, I know, maybe they'd even reward you. And I don't blame you for thinking of it... But when I saw you last night, I felt I already knew you more than anyone else. So I had to write to you.

I'm Hya, I'm the one who asked for your name. I saw you go back into your room after the alarm. If you want to talk, I'm in Unit 1A across the way. You can write on the back of this paper (pen enclosed) and return it under my door.

Make sure you don't get too close and don't let anyone see you.

Hyacinth.

The room came back into focus around her; her floor, her bed, her window, all appeared again. Rumer realised she didn't want to be here any more. She wanted her room to fade into the background again, and be pulled into that avenue of distraction the letter provided. She wanted to be a denizen of Hya's devices.

She reached over to the pen and grabbed it greedily, this time not with her sleeve but her exposed hand. She turned over the paper to the blank side and started to write uncontrollably. Her hand seemed to move the pen for her as her thoughts poured out onto the page.

Hyacinth, That's a nice name. Sorry for my handwriting, I haven't used a pen since I was little, hope it's readable! It's funny, I feel like I can be honest with you too, even though we only said a few words to each other last night. I wished I'd talked to you more, I must have looked so timid. I didn't know how to feel about your letter. It scared me, I'll admit it, but I was amazed too, I couldn't believe it, the nostalgia, handwritten, as well. I'm rambling, sorry, I don't know what to say... Anyway, I do want to talk, yes, I would like that. Rumer, Unit 2A —well, you know that already.

Enthralled by new verve, she folded the paper back up and rushed to leave her room and out into the corridor. She couldn't wait for Hya to read her response. But she halted, seeing the sign once again on the inside of her door. It stared at her and down its nose at her, its familiar words condemning her.

STAY SAFE. STAY INSIDE. STAY IN YOUR ROOM.
FOR YOUR OWN SAFETY AND THE SAFETY OF OTHERS.

Her confident flourish was quashed. She fretted again about the paper and the pen, and them being in her room. She had used them too now, irrefutably. She looked at the sign, then back down to the letter she clutched in her game hand. She took another deep breath, took a stride towards the door and opened it.

Hya had finished reading Rumer's reply. She writes as someone might speak, she thought: a stream of consciousness, unedited, she found it refreshing. Hya had been apprehensive about reaching out. Though she'd judged Rumer to be trust worthy, it was always hard to tell, especially these days. So she'd been relieved to find the letter just inside her door.

Hya lay on her bed, holding the piece of paper over her. She turned to her side and pulled herself over the edge. She folded it up several times and stuffed it under her mattress. Then she reached under the bed and drew out a notepad, her other hand reached to her bedside lamp, where she took a pen from its stem. She rolled onto her back again, put the pad on her raised knees and started to write her response.

> *Rumer,*
> *Call me Hya, it will save you some ink.*
> *I don't know what to say either. Now we can say what we like, it somehow seems harder to find the right words...*
> *But, I guess, I want to know, what do you think of all this? It's hard to actually speak to people about it, isn't it? Do you think all this will ever end? We've been like this now for more of our lives than we haven't. And I'm sure there's more to it. What's really going on outside? Can it really be that bad?*
> *Tell me I'm not crazy, right? Tell me this isn't normal...*
> *Hya.*

She looked over what she'd written and she felt an urge to rip it up and start over. She should write something else, she thought, something anodyne, benign. This was far too risky.

She considered for a moment.

No, she wouldn't change it. This is what she wanted to say. She needed to know how Rumer felt, how *anyone* else felt.

She tore off the page, folded it, pressing over the crease. She crept from her room, and checking the corridor, she crossed to the other side, seeing the sign again on the outside of Rumer's door.

NO ENTRY UNLESS YOU ARE THE REGISTERED OCCUPIER.
IF YOU SEE ANYONE SUSPICIOUS, PLEASE REPORT THEM IMMEDIATELY TO YOUR SAFETY TEAM.

Hya smirked at it and slid the new note under the door. Then she paused, staring at the doorway for a moment. She imagined Rumer behind it and wondered what she might be doing. How easy would it be just to knock, she thought. But she knew she couldn't, they would know, and Rumer would be corrected, or worse.

She shook off the impulse and returned quietly to her room.

Later that day, Hya found a second reply by her door as she woke from a nap. Impressed with Rumer's promptitude, she picked up the letter and took it back to bed. Lying in her same customary position, she held the letter out in front of her.

Hya, No, you're not crazy, I feel it too, it all seems ridiculous somehow, like some kind of spiteful prank being played on us. But I think no one wants to admit it. I think everyone wants to carry on believing, shut their eyes and hope it might go away. How did all this even happen anyway? How did it get this bad and no one did anything? We were just kids so we didn't know any better. But the rest, the adults, they just went along with it, no questions asked. But just maybe there's still a chance, right, maybe it's never too late, maybe one day it won't be like this. We can at least hope, right? Tell me we can at least do that... Rumer.

3
THE OTHERS

A cold autumn persisted. Hya's privation was only made bearable by her burgeoning liaison with Rumer. Their letters invoked an innocence that endeared Hya to share far more openly than she would online. Sometimes, she had to remind herself not to be so forthcoming; for at any moment, Rumer could be tempted by the potential rewards from perfidy. Irregardless, Hya's outlook had completely changed from their exchanges. She no longer felt alone in her cynicism and in her scepticism for what had happened in the city, and she no longer had to struggle with ostracism and doubt herself. Now she knew there were others like her and perhaps, she dared to fantasise, maybe everyone was like her.

Encouraged by this first interaction, Hya decided she would write to the rest of the building in the hope of similar outcomes. There were ten units in the block. Hya had seen every occupier outside during the fire alarm, but had only seen Rumer enter *her* room. So she did not know who lived in which unit.

She started on the ground floor, where there were two more units, and she slipped notes under the doors of both of them. She worried again, but soon received one reply, allaying half of her concern.

The first to write back was Ophelia. Her and Hya shared the same apartment as it was originally, now segmented into two. From her letter, Hya placed her as the older woman from when they'd been outside. If it was her, Ophelia had stayed mostly in the middle of them, the others naturally safeguarding her. She had a poetic, fanciful style of writing, which Hya found quaint. It was a style far removed from anything she would read online nowadays.

Dearest Hyacinth,
How wonderful to see handwriting, how sophisticated. But how on earth did you come to have pen and paper, I wonder? I

remember when we had nothing but pen and paper, of course. You know, I was moved to this city over a decade ago. It wasn't safe outside. But it can be a challenge to be grateful sometimes, when life is as it is here. I do miss the countryside.

As much as I appreciate your letter, I am a little perturbed that you have forbidden items, is this all quite safe, dear? Won't they find out? It doesn't bother me so much but for the sake of the rest of you...

Soon I will be seventy, you know, and I will be taken to the outskirts. I shudder at the thought. From the stories I have heard, I have little hope of a pleasant retirement.

Enough of me, though. Thank you for writing, Hyacinth. I would of course be delighted to keep writing to one another. Like I say, I have very little left to lose now.

Yours,
Ophelia.
Unit 1B.

The other ground floor unit replied soon after, calming Hya's remaining nerves. Talon had written to her. She placed *him* as the middle aged man from the outside; he hadn't engaged the guards but had helped shield the injured. He introduced himself as a former city worker, living here and in this building most of his life. He once had the whole apartment to himself before it's subdivision, so he felt the imposition of the smaller space more than anybody. He too shared his dismay for the situation they all found themselves.

Hyacinth,

Thanks for your message, not sure how secure this is though. Yes, it was interesting being outside, wasn't it? Very odd being next to other people for a change, the first time in as long as I can remember anyway.

I've been in the city my whole life, I can't believe what has become of it. I used to work here, back when people used to work of course. I even had this whole apartment to myself back in those days. Then they came and changed everything, cut my flat in two! It's so small now, I hate it. What I'd give for a bigger apartment??

But yes, certainly happy to talk to other people, maybe I'll even finally find out who they moved in next to me.
Talon.
Unit 2B.

Hya, spurred on by only positive receipts so far, moved on to the first floor. Now feeling more incautious, she slid letters under the doors of all four units up there, all at once.

The first to reply was Ever, from the first room closest to the stairs. From *his* letter, she guessed he was one of the younger ones from outside, perhaps the one who had provoked the guards; the one who had been struck on the elbow. Ever seemed less critical of the state of the city than the others. He appeared to have largely accepted it and was even somewhat defensive of it. Hya thought that perhaps being so young, he wouldn't have known, or at least remembered, living under any different conditions than the ones imposed upon him now, so he wouldn't think them so aberrant. Ever was not so hardened, or as weary as the other two. In his letter, he came across as enthusiastic and even a little excitable.

Hi Hya,

Amazing! A letter, very cool. I've never seen one before, well, in real life. What made you think of the idea? Kinda risky, though? Not sure you should be doing this.

But yes, it was fun being outside for a change, but I guess it's back to reality now, back to doing our bit. It's not so bad really, it's good in a lot of ways, don't you think.

Ok, sure, I suppose there's no real harm in it, so just keep me posted, Unit 3A. I'll defo write you back.
Cheers!
Ever.

Next to reply was Cleo, from the unit opposite Ever. Hya recognised a similarly youthful style in *her* letter, so she placed Cleo as the youngest of the women she'd seen outside.

Hey Hya,

Great letter, I had no idea what this was at first. I can't remember the last time I wrote something down, not since I was little anyway.

I'm glad you're safe and the others are too. We just need to keep our heads down, don't we, stick to what they say and we'll be okay. Let's keep it up!

Yes, of course, I'd like to be involved. So who else is in? I want to say hello *to everyone, it's like a secret society or something.*

Cleo, Unit 4A.

Hya guessed both Cleo and Ever had only just turned twenty, perhaps were even just shy of it. So she was saddened by what she read as their ambivalence towards the city and all that it had done to them. She imagined they'd been habituated their whole lives into acceptance of it and now they suffered from something of a callow naivety. They weren't only supine but seemed supportive of their restrictions, even arguing for them.

Hya hypothesised that having been exposed to the conditioning of the city for a much greater fraction of their lives than the others, any intolerance would have been disabused from them. Moreover, their growing up with screens all around them; their existing almost entirely in a digital realm, rendered them incapable of separating the digital world they occupied most of the time from the physical one they actuated. And therefore, they were happy with living in the fantasy they had created for themselves online, it simply replacing their flawed reality.

Annia replied next, from the unit next to Ever. Hya was fairly certain she was the second person to be struck by the guards, on the back. She thought her and Annia were of similar ages, nearly thirty perhaps. So with youth as her ally, Annia's back would likely have already healed from the blow. Hya could not abide those who let injury slow them down. She couldn't glean much from Annia's letter, it was so concise. But she had asked a very significant question, one which Hya would think about a lot.

Hya,
Unit 3B.
Thank you for the letter. It was very nice.
What is your ultimate goal for all of this though?
Thanks,
Annia.

Finally, and completing the four units on the first floor, was Caius, next door to Cleo. Hya knew he was the older male from outside, perhaps approaching Ophelia's age. There was something oddly familiar about the tone of his letter. She found herself amused by it. His words read with a self-effacing waggishness, but it wasn't always obvious if the humour was intended. Then Hya realised why it was so familiar: Caius sounded like her own father. He had the same dry wit, the same lumbering raillery — that was the way he used to bond with someone. She found herself reading Caius' letter, imagining it in her father's voice.

Dear Hya,
Well, well, a letter, written by hand. I'm surprised anyone can remember how to write...or read for that matter. I'm Caius, a golden oldie, so if you ever want a story that starts with, in my day, *then you know where to come.*
Fire alarm? There was a fire alarm? No, just joking, I'm not quite that deaf yet, I still have some thing left in this thick skull.
So are we writing love letters or something? I thought you young'uns used all your clever phones and things these days?
I'll join in, as long as no one sends me nothing soppy. I suppose congratulations are in order for turning our building into the speakeasy of letter writing.
Bye for now, neighbour.
Caius.
Unit 4B.

With eight of them now involved, and nothing yet to discourage her, Hya continued on to the top floor. There were just two units up there; one apartment built into the eves of the building. She delivered notes to each of them.

Otto was the first to reply and after reading *his* letter, Hya realised she'd been mistaken: it was not Ever who had been first hit by the guards but Otto. She knew it was him straight away. His letter was blunt, impassioned and fulminating of the city; it even emboldening Hya to thoughts of further mischief. She'd also noticed how Otto had abbreviated her name: he'd called her *Hy*. And this brought back memories for her from before the last days of school, where *Hya* had been one syllable too long for the youthful lingo of her classmates.

Otto - 5A.
Sometimes I forget there's other people around, just through this floor and on the other side of these walls, but then something like this reminds you, doesn't it; there's tons of people around, isn't there, everywhere, just like me. The city? Yes, I hate it, I hate all of this. I think we all do, but no one dares say anything. They're cowards, all of them, lazy cowards, telling themselves they're so good, they're kidding themselves. I don't know where everyone's mettle went, Hy. It's embarrassing. We should do something. This is a good start.

And then finally, there was Draven, the last remaining resident of the block to reply. He was a little older, perhaps in his mid to late forties. He had stayed mostly in the background outside and she had barely registered him. His letter was even shorter than Annia's and there was even less Hya could infer from it. She wasn't even sure if it was a polite decline or a tacit assent to be involved. But his brevity hooked Hya and she was intrigued by him. She chose to keep him updated anyway.

Hya,
Thank you for your letter.
Your group of writers sounds very interesting.
Draven (5B).

And with this, all nine of them had now replied to her. Hya was confident she had placed the faces from the outside with their corresponding letters. They were all united only by the tenuous link of their experience together during the fire alarm and the common roof they shared over their heads. Hya considered whether she had burdened them with secrecy and malfeasance. But her reaching out hadn't seemed to irk them. In fact, from reading their letters, they seemed somewhat revitalised, perhaps even unshackled from some of their perfunctoriness.

The group had come together again like they had outside in the cold; them, against the city. How had Draven referred to them in his letter, she thought: *writers*, yes, that was it, that was the perfect name for them. The Writers, that is what they'd be.

4
THOUGHTS OF ESCAPE

The last month of autumn had arrived and the group were now acquainted with one another through the letters. Hya had introduced them, then encouraged them to write directly to each other using the paper they now had. The others did, and were soon able to also put names to the faces they'd seen outside. Now when Hya received letters back, there were multiple sets of handwriting on them, showing this additional discourse between the others. She would read it all with interest and was able to learn more about each of the group. She noticed in particular how Cleo and Ever's evasive tenor was beginning to change. The two of them had heard the stories from the others about life before the changes. It was an epoch they had almost no memory of. *Their* history only started with the protests, anything from before was missing from their education.

Furthermore, Hya began to notice some letters returned to her with parts torn off, so she guessed there were now private conversations going on between some of the others, using these bits of paper they'd commandeered. She had her suspicions as to who had siphoned paper; Ophelia for one, Talon another, and possibly Cleo, a third. She understood their desire for privacy but with her paper now strewn all over the building, she could no longer account for all of it. It seemed her own system was outgrowing her.

Despite this, when there was ever a issue that concerned the whole group, the others would still loyally notify Hya first. She would then write a circular if there was something worthy of report, addressing the letter to, *The Writers*. This would then be passed from one unit to the next, until everyone had seen it.

The uptake of the letters had far exceeded Hya's expectations, she could never have imagined that such a communication network could exist away from the arbitration of the city. The letters had allowed the group to vent without its censure or risk of being docked; they were unfiltered, unexpurgated, and they couldn't be doctored, *or* deleted.

But Hya was still unsettled.

Though the letters had no digital footprint, the building itself had been long overdue its search. She backed *herself* to hide her own pens and paper effectively but she doubted the others. She was sure the guards would find *something* and this indulgence would end.

Annia, in her first letter to Hya, had asked her what her *ultimate goal was from all of this*, imputing to Hya a desire for something more than just small talk between tenants. Though she might pontificate, Hya knew the real answer, and really she'd known since the day the fire alarm had sounded. But what she desired most was far more consequential than the mild misdemeanours the group had offended so far. She was cautious and needed to clarify her thoughts. There was only way she knew how.

She took out her notepad and a pen and started to write.

There was still only one recipient she trusted enough to share her whole mind with.

Rumer,

I want to tell you something. I want to explain why I wrote to you, why I wrote to all of you.

When I saw everyone outside together, I had a feeling I'd never experienced before. I saw us do things together we would never dream of doing on our own. But because we were side by side, we did them. We talked back to the guards like they were just one of us, we stepped to them like we weren't afraid, we even fought with them when it could never be a fair fight.

But that's how they subdue us, isn't it, that's how they control us; they atomise us, and separate us. When we're alone, we're weak, but when we are united, we're strong.

Ru, I'm going to try and get us out of here, everyone! I want us all to be rid of the city for good. But we all need to go together to make it work. I'm not sure when, or how, but somehow I will, I'll save all of us.

Hya.

She surveyed what she'd written, wondering how Rumer would react reading it. She wondered how *all* the others might react to it, and to her plan. Would they even consider something so drastic? Hya's confidence in them would be helplessly exposed. Her faith was waning. Could she really trust all of them?

But Hya was running out of time. The guards would come soon. Whether to search the block or to apprehend Ophelia, they would come. *Her* time was running out too. Hya could not let Ophelia spend her final years in misery in care. If her scheming cost her, or any of the group, Hya could not forgive herself.

She couldn't falter any longer, she had to act. However the group might react; reject her or betray her, she had to tell them.

She tore off another sheet of paper and wrote at the top, *To The Writers*.

5
PLANS OF ESCAPE

Dearest Hya,

You are wonderful, my dear, to think of me. Of course, I would love to join you. You know my feelings on my hastening extraction from here, I would do whatever I could to avoid it. I don't want to die in one of those dreadful care houses.

Forgive my negativity though, but isn't it even more dangerous outside the city? How on earth will we survive out there?

Anyway, I do trust you, Hya, that you know what you are doing and what you might be starting.

And why not *go? It can't be any worse than this, can it. Let me live freely one last time. I'll go as far as my ancient legs can carry me. I may be slow, but I will follow you.*

Yours,
Ophelia.

Ophelia was the first to respond to Hya's letter. In it, she had asked the group if they would be willing to join her, join her in attempting to escape the city. Hya was lifted by this first response, not least, because she now felt closer to a day when her and Ophelia might actually meet.

Then a second reply soon came, from Caius, also in the affirmative. He assented with much more chary however. His frequent pokes at his own old age had not been entirely in jest; he *was* concerned his senility might impair the rest of them, and endanger them.

Further responses were then received, Annia replying next, also agreeing to join them. Then in quick succession, Ever, Cleo, Otto, Talon and even Draven, who hardly wrote, all responded. And all were willing to come.

Talon, in his reply, had also pre-empted the others, already proposing a possible plan of action for them.

Hya, it's very brave to even have that thought of escaping in your head. They don't like those kinds of thoughts. The city is a troublesome place but you need to be extra careful on the outside. From what they say, it's even more unsafe.

But I'm up for the challenge. I know I can help too, I know a way out of here. I said I worked for the city before...well, it was in transport, and before that, I was a bus driver. I know, quite the skill set. When the buses were stopped for good, the stations were abandoned and left mostly as they were. The buses themselves would have been processed of course, but I reckon they'd still be functional. And I happen to still have a set of master keys they never bothered checking. I'm sure I could put some life back into one of them and I can drive us to the outskirts.

You'd have to come up with some plan to get passed the perimeter though but —

Hya dropped the letter.

The perimeter, how could she have forgotten it!

She pictured it from the images online: the defensive barrier that belted the city. No one had ever breached it; its precipice was too high, its walls too thick, and guards were stationed at every measure of it. It protected the city from the outside, no one could get in. But no one could get out either. It was impregnable, daunting, and it humbled Hya.

Her plan seemed futile now.

Another night passed, and as a little morning light managed to filter into her room, curbing her pessimism, Hya wrote to the group again. Despite her deflation, and her own scepticism of Talon's plan, she felt she owed him an audience for his endeavour and she reluctantly presented his idea to the others. If nothing else, she thought, it might at least kick start a brain storming.

The plan was quickly shot down as Hya had anticipated. Ophelia, replying promptly as ever, was the first to reject it, and was trenchant with her rebuke.

Dear Hya,

Thank you for that, I haven't laughed so hard in years. Me? The action hero, hurtling through the city. On a bus!

What are we going to do, fly over the perimeter on this bus of his?

Sorry, I do quip, I trust you won't share this with the poor man, I would hate for him to read my sententious drivel.

Yours,
Ophelia.

Hya received more responses, most of them sharing similar indignation for Talon's plan. Otto was one of them. But in his cross examination, he had asked if Talon's expertise extended beyond the buses and included the trains. And at the mention of trains, Hya immediately thought of the city subway and intuitively she knew, this was the way to go.

She forwarded Otto's enquiries onto Talon, adding her own thoughts about the subway, and asked him if he could ratify this new direction. He replied.

Hi all,

Do I know the subway? Of course I know the subway, I know everything about transport! It was my whole life.

The station near here; they never bother guarding them, they never even secured them. If we can make it down there, then sure, it might work.

Mind you, I don't know what's down there now...might be runaways, vermin, loose cables, all sorts, you never know. And no power remember, we won't be able to see where we're going. And you're talking days to hike anywhere, not hours!

But yes...it's a good idea actually, I wish I'd thought of it!
Talon.
P.S. No one fancies the bus then??

Hya felt energised by their progress, the beginnings of a workable plan seemed to be materialising.

Talon's response was then circulated and shortly after, Hya received a letter from Annia. It was as salient and pointed as usual.

Hi Hya,
Concerning the light in the subway: we can use our phone torches for light down there, they should last long enough if we take turns and use them sparingly. And, you should ask Talon where the end stations are; is there one which comes out beyond the perimeter?
Just a thought.
Annia.

Hya passed on Annia's letter to Talon and Talon knew of three such stations that would likely be outside the perimeter, one of which connected with a line they could take from their nearest station.

So a feasible plan had at last been formulated. It held up to scrutiny, it was realistic, and even felt attainable.

Hya mulled over all the letters one final time. She pulled them all out from under her mattress, scoured through them to see if she might have missed something, if a better plan hid in them somewhere.

She concluded it didn't.

Hya was stressing at the thought of actually going through with anything. But she knew she couldn't deliberate any longer. She lay on her bed, in the same position as always, took out her notepad and composed one last letter to the group. At the top of the page, she'd copied a street map that Talon had drawn for her, showing the route on foot to reach the subway — in case they didn't know. Then below this, she wrote out her final instructions.

To The Writers,
Tomorrow night, we leave as soon as darkness comes. As mentioned, we must go one at a time to avoid any suspicion.

Remember, we go in order of room number, just wait for the sound of the door next to you.

Use the map above and go straight to the subway station. Don't stop, keep going down, they won't be able to track our phones down there. We will meet on the mezzanine floor.

Bring whatever supplies you can, we'll be underground for two to three days. Don't forget to charge your phones fully; as Annia says, we need them for light down there. It will be pitch black otherwise.

I will see everyone tomorrow.
Good luck.
Hya.

6
UNDERGROUND

They reconvened in the subway after leaving the block one by one. They'd traversed several streets to reach the station and found, as Talon had described, nothing to stop them entering. As each had come down to the mezzanine level, they'd gathered around one prominent figure, knowing it was her. The group waited for her to speak.

'We won't have much time here,' Hya said to them quietly, just making them out by the light seeping down from the entranceway above, 'So we have to start moving. Talon, Otto and I will take the lead. Remember Talon knows the layout, so we're following him, okay.'

Hya had clocked Otto as the group had collected underground. Her prejudgement of him matched what she saw now, so she was confident in his agency and reliability. She'd decided she would delegate to him when needed.

She gestured forward to him and he moved into the dark, out of sight from the others. Then he turned his phone torch on and a fence appeared before them. Otto ran his hand over part of it, then lifted up a section, dragging it towards him. A gap was left, enough for the group to slip through one at a time.

'See, easy, told you they didn't bother securing anything,' Talon said, satisfied with himself.

Hya glanced at him as she went through the gap first. Otto held open the fence, shining his phone light as the others followed. The entrance opened out into a large foyer, with ticket machines to the left, and a seated waiting area to the right, straight ahead were stairs and escalators leading down.

Talon stood at the front of the group. They all waited for his direction. He sized up the area, taking his time. The rest of them flirted anxious glances at each other. Hya received the most looks.

'Talon?' Otto finally challenged, flashing his light towards him.

'It's…it's…,' he mumbled, '…this way,' and he flailed his arm out in one direction.

The group funnelled down one of the stairways and found themselves in another large hallway.

The air was close down here and Hya noticed how restricted her breathing was. She hadn't thought at all about this and she wondered how many other factors she hadn't considered.

The hallway bifurcated and Talon, without needing to think this time, led them down one of the tunnels. Otto, now at the back of them, tried to keep the group in his and the only light.

'It's down here, keep going for a while,' Talon announced.

Hya had taken the lead as they walked, with Talon just behind her. The group had broken into pairs as the tunnel narrowed.

Hya turned to check with Talon if they should continue on but then realised he was no longer just behind her. She stopped, the others came passed her and carried on ahead. Otto was the last to pass.

'Otto, your light,' she said to him, holding her arm out.

He handed her his phone and she shone it back down the tunnel. Talon was standing there. She felt a shiver and suddenly she felt cold. She could see her own breath like mist in front of her.

'Talon?' she said.

He did not respond. He was looking down at the ground.

The others, realising Hya had stopped, came back and grouped around her.

'Talon?' she enquired again.

Talon lifted his head up slowly and looked back at her.

'Hya,' he said, in a hushed voice.

The light flickered, Hya could only partially see his face.

'It's not that way,' he said.

'What?' Hya responded.

'It's not that way,' Talon repeated, 'We have to go back and take the other turn.'

'You said this way?' said Otto accusingly.

'I know, but it's not. You have to go back, it's a dead end that way.'

Otto rolled his eyes theatrically.

Hya moved closer to Talon, waving the others to follow her.

'What's going on Talon?' she said.

'I...,' he started, 'I told them.'

'Told who?' Otto interjected.

Then what was happening started to dawn on Hya and the others.

'I told you,' Talon said, 'I hate that unit, its so small. They offered me a bigger one and...a-a TV, and-and actual food, and...whatever else I wanted. They...they wanted to catch you in the act...' He hung his head. 'I'm sorry.'

There was silence. The group were frozen, realising Talon's betrayal. They felt trapped, powerless.

Hya was the first to react. She passed the phone light back to Otto, went to Talon and grabbed his jacket with both hands. Otto kept the light on them.

'Show us the way, Talon. You said there was another turn, you mean the last one? Take us there,' she urged him.

He did not respond.

Otto went for him suddenly, his light flashing around the tunnel as he came forward. Hya thought he might strike him. She lifted her hand.

'Wait,' she asked of him, thinking this wouldn't help.

Otto paused, but was on edge.

Hya looked back at Talon.

'Look, you can still help us,' she implored, 'You want to help us, I know you do, you wouldn't have confessed otherwise. So please, Talon, help us,' and she shook his jacket again.

Talon looked up and saw the concern in Hya's eyes. He looked over at the rest of them, they were all watching him. They looked desperate, helpless and scared. Talon saw them for what they were now, and realised their humanity. He felt ashamed for what he had done.

A rumbling was heard above them. Then muffled voices followed. Guards had arrived at the station entrance.

Talon was alarmed into action. He had decided, his conscience gave him no other choice.

'Okay, follow me. Now!' he shouted and turned from the group, hurrying back down the tunnel.

The group followed hesitantly.

'Follow exactly where I go,' he shouted, 'Keep up, we don't have much time.' He took out his own phone to light the way.

The group broke into a canter, Talon's light now ricochetted around the tunnel as they ran.

Ophelia and Caius were struggling to keep up. Annia and Ever slowed and offered a shoulder each to Caius. Otto came back also and picked up Ophelia. They ran to catch the others.

The group were moving towards the noise now. It grew louder and all of Hya's instincts told her to turn around. Any moment they would see the torches, masks, and armour, moving inexorably towards them. She wondered if this was another trap, set by Talon, but she followed him regardless, having no choice but to entrust the fate of the group to his apparent change of heart.

They came to the same junction they had passed earlier. Talon lead them down the other path this time.

Running away from the noise now, Hya immediately felt relieved, and vindicated.

They continued for a while, then Talon slowed to a stop. He shone his light onto a wall to the side.

'Through here,' he said.

There was a hatch, with a row of bars across it.

'That looks tiny,' Otto said, catching up to him, Ophelia still in his arms.

'It's a conduit, for the workers, it'll take you through to the other line,' Talon explained, turning a lever and unlocking it. The hatch opened.

The group were gathered by the wall but stayed where they were, just watching him.

'The safeties won't see it,' he insisted, 'Come on, go through.'

Hya saw the others hesitating, she couldn't fault them. But still she kept her faith in him and started to usher them through, knowing they needed her assurance.

They all passed into the conduit and continued on ahead. Hya followed behind them. She had taken a few steps, then realised... She turned round. Talon wasn't beside her. He was stationary, still on the other side of the hatchway.

'Talon?' she said.

He was looking at the ground again.

'Don't you dare —' Hya started, and dashed towards him.

Talon closed the hatch instantly and it slammed shut before Hya could reach it. He turned the lever again, locking it between them.

Hya tried to pull open the hatch but she couldn't, and she hit the bars in frustration. She looked at him.

'Don't go,' she begged, 'Come with us, they'll forgive you, I promise you they will.'

Talon looked back at her, his face distraught.

'I have to go back and make-make sure they don't follow,' he said, his voice trembling, 'I have to make up-make up for what I've done. I'll say, I'll say you didn't come down here...you're out on the streets, I-I came down here alone...'

'Just come with us,' she implored him again, 'No one will mind, we'll get over this, we will.'

'I can't,' he said firmly. A calm had settled over him, his mind was made.

Hya lashed at the bars in frustration again and ripped back on the hatch as hard as she could. Still it didn't move. She keeled over holding the bars, exerted, breathless from the effort. She whispered to herself, *but the group has to stay together.* She drooped further downwards, still griping the bars; disconsolate and dejected.

'Listen,' Talon said, seeing her attention was fading, 'Listen to me,' still she didn't respond, 'Hya!' he hissed.

She flinched and finally lifted her head to him. He gave her instructions.

'When you come out to the main tunnel, turn right. You then stay left, always left, understand?' She nodded, closing her eyes to concentrate. 'You'll pass under fifteen stations, keep count of them, the sixteenth is the outstation, it should be beyond the perimeter. And you can come up to the surface then, okay.'

Hya opened her eyes and looked at him. She opened her mouth to try to persuade him to change his mind again, but Talon didn't let her speak.

'Go now, hurry!' he ordered.

Hya and Talon paused for a brief moment, looking at each other, trying to put to memory the others' face permanently. They both knew Talon's fate.

He thought to say something else but then only gave a slight nod, and this spoke everything for him. Talon turned and ran back down the tunnel until Hya could no longer see him.

7
CONVERSATIONS IN THE DARK

They had walked in silence so far, the events of the journey had fully engaged them and it hadn't even occurred to them yet to talk to one another. Now in the calm and the stillness of the tunnel, they were beginning to appreciate how improbable their situation was. For the first time, they marvelled at the living, breathing and tangible human beings walking beside them. They shared looks with each other to remark on the surreality; asking, how was it possible they were this close; close enough to touch, to talk and to hear. Inevitably and ineluctably, words soon escaped several lips. Others then joined in and the light din of conversation had descended.

The width of the tunnel around the tracks had once again restricted the group into pairs. Hya and Otto were at the front. They remained quiet even after overhearing the others; their talking hadn't prompted them to do the same.

Hya would occasionally look back at Rumer who was walking behind them, feeling she might prefer to walk alongside *her* instead.

After a while though, Hya and Otto too would permit a few words between them, though they limited themselves to talk of the mission only, neither wanting to provoke circumstance just yet, they were still well within city limits.

'How long do you think to get there, Hy?'

'We've only come passed one station so far, so...it's hard to say...two more days, maybe.'

'What about the outside? You think it's safe?'

'I don't know what to think any more, Otto. It feels like we can't believe anything we think we know any more. I wonder if anyone's really out there, if there's any danger at all.'

There *was one* moment of levity shared between the two of them that they *couldn't* help. When they spoke of the supplies that the others had brought with them, they'd noticed how Ever and Cleo, the two youngest of the group, had brought nothing at all, despite Hya's instruction to do so.

'They must have thought this was one of those old school trips,' Otto joked, 'That we'd bring a packed lunch for them or something.'

Hya smirked and said, 'Yes, at each station we'd take a roll call; Ever? Cleo?' she pretended.

'Present, Sir!' Otto joined in, chuckling.

Hya laughed.

Rumer could hear the sudden conviviality ahead and she lost interest in her own conversation with the person next to *her*. She wondered what they were laughing at and was frustrated she wasn't part of the joke.

The group had largely gravitated towards those of a similar age, so Rumer was walking beside Annia. Annia was not a prolific letter writer but had contributed invaluably. She had made the suggestion to use their phone lights whilst underground and even more importantly, had brought up if they could potentially resurface beyond the perimeter. Annia enjoyed reading the letters far more than writing them. Due to her propensity for watching TV series, she viewed them like another unfolding drama she could follow. She would envisage relationships among the group and speculate on all their interactions. As each new letter arrived, she was intrigued to read the latest episode.

Annia was on this, her favourite topic of TV and Rumer had listened along sportingly so far, volunteering when she could what she had or had not seen also. As Otto and Hya laughed in front, Annia looked at Rumer to see her staring ahead at them. Annia continued talking and Rumer turned back to her, then began nodding overtly. Annia could see in Rumer the wide eyed vacancy of someone who wasn't listening and she paused mid sentence. This made Rumer *aware* that she had been caught in her pretence and she flushed with embarrassment. Then Annia felt guilty for *causing* this embarrassment, she would have happily moved on to save Rumer's blushes.

Annia had noticed this wasn't the first time Rumer's eyes had been fixed on Otto and Hya up ahead. It hinted at an affection Rumer had for one of them. Annia was surprised to feel a pang of jealousy at the thought it might be Otto.

'Sorry, it's just,' Rumer said after realising her moment of inauthenticity, 'it's just so weird, you know, talking to another human...actually in the flesh.'

Annia, amused at Rumer's deflection, leapt at the chance to rib her.

'Yes, well, some humans are better in the flesh than others,' she mocked, nudging Rumer's arm and nodded at the two in front. She then winked at Rumer with a smile, hoping this might diffuse any awkwardness. Rumer paused, then smiled back at Annia coyly.

Following behind *them*, were Ever and Cleo, the aforementioned two youngest members of the group. They had shared letters privately back in the building, Cleo having torn paper off from the main circulation. They were continuing where they'd left off; inane, comforting chatter about anything and everything was bouncing between them.

They were full of smiles and hung on the others' words, eager for their turn to respond. Their peppy conversation filled them with unfamiliar feelings of joy and they realised these sensations were only available because they were here together. They were beginning to notice what a difference this made.

Presently, they were speaking of food they could remember from their childhoods.

'Do you remember pizza?' Cleo asked.

'Of course,' Ever responded, 'What was your favourite topping?'

'Mm...it was so long ago, I think I just liked plain...cheese, I suppose.'

'Ah, what about crisps? What was your favourite flavour?'

'Barbecue flavour.'

'Barbecue?' Ever gave a quizzical look.

'Yep, you?'

'Mm, salt and vinegar,' Ever said, with a neotenous grin.

They were unfiltered, asking whatever came to them, and were enjoying the cheery company of the other. Yet still, the two of them felt far more recusant than the others to be here. They were unable to shed a feeling of guilt for deserting the city. But in the presence of the other, they could shroud themselves in temporary joviality and this mostly untroubled them. With the other, they were able to stave off thoughts about the seriousness of their actions which might depress them and they could convince themselves for now, this was just a carefree adventure, for which there would be no repercussions.

And lastly, at the back of the group, were the three eldest; Caius and Ophelia side by side, and Draven just behind them — it was his turn to provide the light. The three of them also reminisced like Ever and Cleo, but they spoke in stories, not through question and answer. They took turns telling each other of their past experiences before the changes. Ophelia was currently sharing a story. She was the oldest of the group, still a few days short of her being relocated to the outskirts. Caius, next to her, thought Ophelia an excellent orator. He would be transfixed as she regaled tales of the past; she was evocative and painted with huge strokes pictures of history. Caius was saddened by the nostalgia he felt but also happy to remember better times. Draven, being a little younger, had no stories of such antiquity, nor the inclination to share them, but enjoyed listening to the other two. He remained mostly silent.

Their reminiscing was cathartic, their stories conveying the longing they had for times they dearly missed. They bonded over these reflections, never losing enthusiasm for each other's contribution and relishing every evocation.

Ophelia could be so performative at times. When she told a story, she would throw her arms out, use funny voices, or exclaim wildly. Sometimes, the rest of the group would hush to hear her and turn an intrigued ear. They had never heard anything quite like it, they couldn't imagine such drama could be conveyed by only words. When Ophelia spoke, everyone wanted to listen.

Cauis, much like Ophelia, also had a voice that carried, but his was coarse and dry. His stories were punchy and funny, but not always intentionally so. At one of his denouements, Caius looked up to see unexpectedly the whole group laughing at what he'd said. Though bemused, he was glad to discover he was so entertaining for them. He had always felt a burden to the group, he was sluggish and had needed help to run before. So when he saw the cheer he had spread, he was happy to know he was contributing, if it was only to humour the rest of them once in a while.

Though they were losing their sense of time, Hya had guessed over a day had passed in the underground. They had come under many stations now and were tiring. Years of incarceration had made the group unhealthy and dormant. They were so used to inactivity, their bodies struggled to adapt to demands now placed on them. The long hike had tested their brittle legs and the stagnant air led to breathlessness, worst felt in the eldest amongst them. They were running low on supplies, especially water. The quantities they had brought were unsubstantial and couldn't sustain them.

The group needed rest.

Hya, seeing them lagging, finally called them to a stop. Some crashed to the floor immediately from exhaustion. Ever and Cleo went dutifully with water and attended to them. Hya, Otto and Annia, *her* phone light now being used, were the only ones left standing and they tabled a discussion between them.

'We've passed under eleven stations, we're well over halfway,' said Hya, 'There can't be that far to go now.'

'They need to rest, Hya,' Annia argued, 'I know it's not ideal, but we can sleep on the ground, just for a bit.'

'But we need supplies, not to stop,' said Otto.

Annia, seeming prepared for this, responded accordingly.

'Yes. I noticed the stations have hardly been touched, I think we can get some supplies from the next station,' she suggested, 'Besides, I don't think we have much choice.' She leant her head subtlety to the other two, indicating Ophelia and Caius who were on the ground; their faces were covered in sweat and they were breathing strenuously.

Hya assessed the suffering group one more time.

'Okay, they can sleep, but not for long,' she compromised, 'But we'll,' - nodding to Otto - 'press onto the next station and we'll come back with what we can find. Everyone else stay here.'

Hya put on her phone light, and she and Otto turned away and continued up ahead.

The group used their bags and their clothes to form makeshift pillows and blankets. They lay tightly together to stay warm but they could still see their breath in the air. When they had settled, Annia turned her phone light off. They slept for a while in the cold and in the darkness of the tunnel, with the sound of mice scampering around them.

They were woken by Otto and Hya's return, Hya's flashing light disturbing them from their respite. The two of them were carrying bags full of food and drink, with what looked like packaged snacks and bottled drinks. Otto strutted proudly towards the others.

'You're welcome, food for everyone,' he said as he handed out the goods to them.

'Where did you get all this?' Ever asked as Otto threw him something.

'Couple of vending machines, even a staff cafeteria with some stuff still left,' flaunted Otto.

Ever caught it, looked down at the packet and turned excitedly to Cleo.

'Look, crisps,' he said, 'Crisps!'

Cleo beamed at him, 'Really! What flavour?' she enquired.

'Oh, just salted,' he replied, slightly disenchanted.

'Ah well,' Cleo said smiling, 'still good though.'

Ever opened the packet and gorged on several handfuls, then paused. He then turned and offered them to Cleo. She took a large handful.

'Thanks,' she said, with a coquettish look.

The group ate what they could, leaving enough for what they thought would be the remainder of their hike. The short rest and sugary food was the tonic they needed. They rose to their feet, packed their belongings away and readied themselves for the rest of the journey.

'Any more stories, Caius?' Otto joked as they started to move. Caius chortled instinctively, coughing slightly after.

They were in higher spirits and the pace they kept was much faster. They went with renewed determination, counting down each station as they went. Their legs still burned, their mouths dry and sore, and their muscles killed from their exertion, but for this leg, and with the end now thinkable, they kept going.

As they continued, they began to remember their fear. They knew nothing, only that danger was waiting for them on the surface. But they doubted these instincts now too, their failing trust in their own feelings was succeeding them. Free from the mental quagmire of the city, they wondered if what they thought they knew, was all untrue. They began to hope as each pictured the beauty of the countryside from what they knew of it. Their imagining spurred them on and they quickened again.

They had passed fifteen stations and it mustn't have been far now to reach the outstation. But their light began to fade; Rumer's phone, now in use, blinked several times, then shut off, depleted. Hya watched as the light went from Rumer's face and they were in darkness again. Hers was the last light they had, all their phones were now used up and dead.

They kept moving, stumbling and feeling for the person in front of them. They tried to keep left, as Talon had instructed, and let the tunnel wall guide them. They trudged unknowingly for a while longer, uncertain. But then eventually, mercilessly, another light emerged ahead. And it could have only been the light of day.

8
DAYLIGHT AND THE RIVER

All they could see was overwhelming white light, their eyes could not yet comprehend it. They saw outlines in the light. Then the outlines became shapes and the white light turned to colours. Now, they saw blue fields beyond them, grey skies above them and a red horizon in front of them. There were no straight edges like in the city, everything before them flowed into each other and swayed with the wind. It wasn't unmoving like the city, and the sapping greys of the buildings had gone too, they were left looking at only all the colours of nature. The red horizon grew and subsumed the sky. It turned golden and the fields washed golden too. Hills were drawn in the moving light, their shadows crept underneath them. The trees were awoken and they stretched out their branches. The hedgerows prickled, the grass; yellow tipped and soft, shimmered. Birds choroused, tip toed along the branches, or soared in display of them, showing off.

The group were mesmerised.

Hya watched them as they gazed over the view that had captured them. She felt accomplished, deriving more satisfaction from *their* reactions than her own feeling of success. In reverential silence, they stood there and watched as the morning settled.

Hya at last interrupted them, their attention slowly turning to her.

'We need to get some distance away from the station just in case,' she said, 'There's no one around here for miles, I guess that's something else they made up. But we should still be cautious. Let's go, they'll be nothing *but* views from here on out.'

The group hiked for the rest of the day. They had walked through fields and through woods and still they'd seen no one, none of the danger they'd been warned of. Eventually, they came out by water, adumbrated by the trees. The day light, though it was much brighter out from under cover, was just beginning to fade.

'What is it?' Ever asked, coming up behind the others.

'The foot of a river,' said Cleo, 'I can see it for miles.'

'It's incredible,' Ever wowed, 'I've never seen anything like it.'

'You've never seen water before?' Otto quipped.

'No, well, only on my phone or, you know, out of a tap.'

Otto laughed and turned to the river, basking in the panorama himself; he'd only seen something like it as a child.

Without any direction from the others, Ever decided to remove his shoes and socks, and walk straight into the water. He waded in up to his knees and looked back at the group.

'It feels amazing, it's all around my ankles,' he announced.

The others smiled encouragingly at him.

Cleo joined him in the water too, making waves around the two of them. Ever then went deeper, the water reaching his waist.

'Change your clothes before night time, Ever, you'll catch your death,' shouted Caius to him, but he wasn't sure if his comment had registered.

Ever cupped some water in his hands and splashed it over his face. He looked back exhilarated.

'It's cold!' he said.

The others laughed.

Cleo copied him, then splashed more over her head.

'It's really nice,' she confirmed.

The rest of the group followed them into the water. Some removed their tops so they could bathe, others just washed their faces and under their arms. But all of them were finally able to refresh themselves after days walking through the dust and dirt of the tunnel.

After some time in the water, they came out to shore, dripping and now rejuvenated. Those who needed to change, did — Otto loaning some clothes to Ever — then they sat in a semi circle facing the water, ready to enjoy the imminent sunset. No words were spoken between them once more. They were tired again, but this time, elated all the same.

Ophelia then struggled to her feet using a branch she had found to lever herself up. A few of the others went to help her but she dismissed them. The group, seeing that she was about to speak, gathered in closer and waited patiently. She settled herself and looked at them. The group could feel the anticipation for her sagely words.

'I am the oldest one of us,' she began, looking over them, 'Unless any of you are remarkably young looking.'

The group smiled cordially at her.

'I've witnessed the world change more than any of you. And how it has, how it has...' She paused. 'It's now unrecognisable to me and, I just don't quite understand how this all could have happened. But it has unfortunately, it has.'

Then she pointed at each of them in turn.

'But us,' she said, 'We've actually done something about it. Us. We did.'

Ophelia spoke carefully, allowing each word to resonate. She then turned and gestured over to the water behind them, then looked back at Ever, who seemed surprised to be singled out.

'Ever, you said you had never seen anything like this before. You're so young, you've probably never even been out of the city, and never seen nature before. Not like this anyway, not *real* nature.'

She then looked away from him, addressing the whole group again, 'Me? I have, I've seen it all. I was an outsider and once, this very river would have been full of life; walkers, hikers, runners, families picnicking, kids playing in the water,' she cupped her ear to the water, 'Can you still hear them playing? Can you hear the echoes of their laughter?'

She looked down to the ground around her feet, taking a moment, assuming a more solemn affect before continuing.

'Then, it all happened. Everyone from the outside was moved into the city. We weren't allowed to live out here, we were told it was too dangerous and that the city would protect us,' she looked back up at them, 'So we were put in tiny rooms and we were told we could never leave them. We were told what we could and couldn't do, and it was a long list. We were separated from each other and we were alone together. And for what? To keep us safe? That's what we were told, wasn't it? We were doing it for our own good, for *our* sake and for the sake of all those around us. Now where are we?'

Ophelia became animated, she pulled out her phone, still dead, from her coat pocket.

'And it's not those awful safeties that control us, no...no number of guards could possibly control us all, and it's not those damned signs everywhere either, no. It's...it's these.'

And she held her phone aloft.

'These control us, these!' she said, shaking the phone above her head, 'We live by them, through them, they tell us what to do, where we can go, who to talk to and what to think. Then, they indulge us, coddle us, distract us and manipulate us, so we don't even notice what's really happening around us.'

She paused again.

'They told us we needed them, that we needed our phones, our TV screens and our internet. They said they would make our lives easier, that we couldn't live without them. So we invited everything that controls us into our lives and into our homes. We welcomed it in and we were even happy for it. We let this all happen. We sat back and we did nothing, as our world collapsed around us.'

She caught her breath. The group were hushed.

Ophelia then took a few steps towards the water.

'So...this is what I think of control...,' she said.

She cocked her arm back and threw the phone into the water. The group sat in silence, moved by Ophelia's words and her action.

The water settled over where the phone had fallen in. Soon the water looked as if it had never been disturbed.

'Well said,' said Hya, breaking the silence, blushing in admiration.

'Wonderful speech,' added Caius.

'Spot on Ophelia,' agreed Ever.

'Yeah, great speech,' Cleo joined in.

Similar sentiments were added by the others.

Otto wasn't sure if Ophelia had meant for them to follow her example, but nonetheless, he too took his phone from his pocket, ran to the water's edge and launched it into the river. It spiralled far into the distance, so far away the group could barely see the plash of it entering the water. Otto was breathing heavily and he realised he had put all his energy into that throw.

Hya watched and then did the same. She looked around at the others, and they saw this as their cue. Rumer laughed and then followed first, throwing *her* phone in. Ever and Cleo did the same, throwing theirs. Then Annia, then Draven, then at last Caius. The phones impressed upon the water and it swayed around correcting itself for a short time after. The group watched it eventually settle.

Everything was still again.

None of them wanted to speak after Ophelia, they saw her as undoubtedly the headline act among them. So they just sat down again in contented quiet. They felt lighter, unburdened, and they felt liberated.

The group stayed until the light drew in, then they looked to Hya for direction once again. Hya felt tired herself now and drained from the responsibility. For the first time, she wanted someone else to make a decision. She no longer had any plans, she hadn't even dared to think about making it this far. She had bottled herself up so tightly, obsessed with escaping, and now that they had, she had nothing left.

Then Annia spoke. Hya looked at her, surprised, and relieved that someone else had.

'We should move and find shelter,' she said, 'It will be too cold out here soon.'

'Yes, it's getting on for winter,' nodded Caius, 'It will be freezing overnight.'

Hya thought about it; something else she hadn't considered: the changing seasons.

'Okay, let's move,' she confirmed, feeling she had to.

The night gradually surrounded them. Any darker and the group wouldn't see shelter if it was right in front of them. Hya felt the cold burrowing into her now. They would have to keep moving all night to stave it off and she wasn't sure if the eldest of the group could survive that.

'Look!' Ever shouted suddenly.

The group stopped and turned. He was pointing into the distance.

'Over there,' he said, gesturing ardently with his arm.

The group looked to where Ever was pointing.

'Where?' Otto shouted.

'There!' Ever said, waving again. He thought pointing was all he could do to help them see, but then he added in hope, 'Smoke.'

The group looked again. And this time they did see; smoke, emanating from beyond a spinney, a glow of light just below it, somewhere behind the trees.

'There must be someone there,' said Otto.

'We should look,' said Ever, glancing at Hya.

Hya thought of the smoke, of the fire and of possibilities. Who was there, outside the city and in the wilderness, she wondered, her interest renewed.

'Yes, let's go!' she said, engaged once more.

And the group went intrepidly towards the smoke.

3
AMICA

1
JAGO RECEIVES A MESSAGE

He heard the faint sound of his phone vibrating from somewhere in his room. He didn't move, he just stared blankly at the ceiling as it rang out. It was a different sound to the regular automated city notices: this was a message from the social, which he hadn't used for a long time.

Despite him having to have it on at all times, Jago's phone was buried under some pile of discarded clothes somewhere on his floor. He didn't want to see it, he only associated it with bad news now.

But over the coming days, he was reminded of the sound of the message by its continuing absence; he'd started to imagine it even when it wasn't there. He began to wonder what other tragic news his phone could bring him and his morbid curiosity outgrew his good intention not to get it. Now he *had* to know who, or what, it was.

Shifting to the end of the bed, he rummaged around along the floor. He found his phone and picked it up.

It was a message he hadn't expected.

No disturbances on the District 7 today. Bit dull...

Jago paused, puzzling about how she could have found him. He read the words again, then once again, mouthing them out this time. Memories from the train came back to him and he found he became sentimental thinking about them. A warmth suffused over him. He felt as if his blood had started to thaw.

But then he began to think, inevitably, of only the worst possible machinations of engaging with her...or whoever it was. Negativity quickly overrode all else, as it usually did. It must be some ploy of the city, he assumed, to entrap him, trick him, perhaps more retaliation for his insolence on the train. Yes, interacting with it would only incriminate him further, he'd decided.

Now reticent to reply, he left his phone wanting once more, deep in the debris of his room.

Several more days came and went and Jago thought of only the message. What if it was really her, he agonised.

His mind became nested with such questions. What had possessed her to approach him on that carriage, and why on earth would she message him now? Scenarios, possibilities were playing out uncontested in his imagination. And whether good or bad, they hurt him, because he knew himself, and he knew he might not allow them even the chance to seed.

His constants, his everyday beckoned him suddenly. But it seemed too cosy, too inviting, and made Jago distrustful of it. If he submitted to its familiar embrace once again, there would be nothing crueller than his own mind's retribution if he should pass up this opportunity for disruption.

He had to at least reply.

He thought for a long while about what to say to her, if it was her, and his thumb hovered over his phone that morning, waiting for him to type.

His reply should be witty, engaging, he thought. It should reference their encounter as she had done. But it couldn't be too obscure, but just clever enough. And it should be in keeping too with what she had said, it should build upon it...

After much deliberation, Jago's thumb lowered and finally, he had replied.

Well, I was busy getting interrupted elsewhere.

She was wandering from the bedroom back to her living room when she heard it. She picked her phone up off her new coffee table and saw that he had messaged. She had fretted for several days over his lack of response; inactivity like that on the social usually did not bode well. Her face lifted as she read the message and was reminded of his audaciousness on the train.

Her shift was starting soon.

She speedily typed a reply and left her apartment.

No interruptions from me, promise.

Jago, still in his bed, heard his phone. He turned over as before, reaching down and retrieving it. He read her message. He couldn't think of anything else to add, she seemed to have closed that particular thread of conversation. He put the phone on his bedside table, savouring his response for now.

He would end up ruminating on what he would say to her for the rest of the day.

Jago had found that, for the first time since the news of his mother had sent him spiralling into his torpor, he had left the confines of his bed. It was now early evening and he had made it as far as the kitchen. He had been docked half his rations for the incident on the train, so he was searching his bereft cupboard for leftover food. He'd been feeling a strange discomfort in his stomach, then remembered it as hunger; a primary cognition that in his malaise he'd nearly forgotten.

He found a stray ration pushed to the very back and took and ate it at the kitchen worktop. The food was old, tasteless and nearly stale, but he didn't care, he was ravenous, and each bite was heaven to his voracious body.

He had placed his phone in front of him. He re-read her message and still couldn't decide where to take the conversation. He was less suspicious of her now, though apart from one extra message, there was nothing really new to confute his concerns. But now he found he was much more worried about not saying something interesting than saying something incriminating.

He looked around his unit for inspiration but nothing volunteered. Then he remembered something else from the train and at last he'd thought of something to ask her.

Is blue your favourite colour?

She'd arrived back to her apartment from work. Dropping her bag down with a weary exhale, she sat down on the sofa and checked her phone. He had messaged again.

She was confused at first by what he'd said, not sure what he was referring to. Then it dawned on her; her trainers, her trainers were blue, the ones she changed into after work. He'd noticed them.

She messaged him back.

No, but what did you think of them?

Jago, still in the kitchen, received her response. He found he didn't need to procrastinate this time.

Yes, they definitely stood out.

She smiled to herself, having bought them for that very reason. For in this otherwise dreary city, *she* was the only thing she could enliven.

She wanted to ask him *why* they stood out, why he had asked her this, and many other things, but she knew the character limit on the messages would hinder her, and the thought of an infinite staccato conversation between them already felt exhausting.

She messaged back without thinking, then put her phone down on the coffee table.

Want to chat?

She was surprised to find herself nervous, this was unlike her, but then just a few moments later, he replied again, and she had no time to consider why.

Sure. Let's talk.

She rearranged the space around her, checking what would be visible on the chat and appraising it carefully for any clues of her work. Then she composed herself, sat upright on the sofa and propped her phone up on the coffee table so the screen could see her. She placed one arm across her knee and the other down by her side. Feeling those unfamiliar nerves again, she took a long breath, then pushed the call button.

Jago had sat down too, in his chair by the bed. He rested his phone on its arm and hunched forward, unsure of how he should sit. He was certain now of the authenticity of the messages and that in any moment, he would see her again.

His phone began to vibrate. He accepted the call. He clasped his hands together in front of him to stop them fidgeting. He blushed, then looked at the screen, the countdown had started.

Ninety nine, ninety eight, ninety seven, ninety six...

He appeared on her screen; hands clasped and hunched forward. She observed him, he looked gaunt and much thinner than on the train, and very pale.

'Hi,' he said, as if he was asking a question.

Jago's screen was still blank, only the countdown was displayed in the corner.

'Are you there?' he said clunkily, 'I can't see anything.'

He waited.

Then finally he heard her.

'Yes, one second, I'm joining now.'

She appeared.

They looked at each other.

She looked exactly how Jago had remembered.

'Easier for us to talk on here, right,' she said, breaking the silence.

'Sure,' replied Jago.

There was another pause.

They both felt the atmosphere somehow sterile, both taken aback by how unspectacular this all seemed. What they had built up to be something monumental, now felt plain. Perhaps they had arrived here too easily. They both felt strangely undeserving of this reunion and were disheartened by its bathos.

But as they continued to look at each other, their feelings slowly changed. They remembered the person opposite them from the train and the fascination of the other returned. Still neither spoke but now the unease had melted away, the intrigue between them rekindled. They were both content in the silence now.

She smirked at first but then broke into a smile, a warmness flushing over her. Jago smiled back with a newly sunned complexion.

'So, my trainers stood out, did they?' she said, asking her foremost question.

'*Trainers*?' he responded, 'Oh yes, you don't see colour like that these days.'

'No,' she agreed.

'Looks like a pretty nice apartment...,' he commented, looking behind her.

'Oh, yeah, it's okay. So what were you doing out?' she added quickly, to change the subject.

'Seeing my mum at the outskirts,' he sighed.

'Oh right, how is she?'

'Yep, she's fine,' Jago dissembled, shifting his eyes away from the screen, 'How about you? Where were *you* going?' he said, similarly moving the chat along.

She was nodding and said, 'Yes, yes, same, seeing family, only way you're allowed out, I suppose.'

'I suppose...'

'You know, I heard they were thinking about ending the families program...not sure how that will go down...,' she wondered, trying to make conversation.

'Oh...right,' Jago mumbled, unsure of himself.

A moment passed.

She moved in closer to the phone.

'So what did you think...on the train, I mean, of me coming over?' She was no longer reclined, but had her elbows on her knees, her hands under her chin. She seemed poised for the response.

'The *train*...,' Jago said, thinking about what to say.

He looked down at the floor, then an unexpected feeling of unrestraint came over him. Perhaps it was testament to her affability, or maybe just recklessness.

'I could hear your footsteps and I didn't dare look,' he said openly, 'I was scared we were too close on the train, we had broken the rules and...we'd get in trouble. But then I looked over at you and you looked like you didn't care, like the rules didn't apply to you. And...I don't know...I...,' he looked up at her on the screen, '...I saw you, when the guard was there, and, I guess, I didn't care either for a moment. And so I stood up to it. It didn't seem to matter what happened to me any more, for once, I just didn't care.'

His eyes darted back to the floor, feeling suddenly as if he had said too much.

She was muted by his candour, she hadn't expected it, especially this early on.

'Hey,' she said so he'd look back up, which he did, 'I understand.'

She smiled again.

Three, two, one, zero.

Their chat ended.

2
JAGO'S DECISION

They continued to talk almost every day throughout the autumn months, always after she'd arrived home from work, though she never mentioned this to him. It became a fulcrum in Jago's day, he could schedule towards it, and around it, and soon, he found himself adhering to some semblance of a routine. He now had the impetus to get up each morning, eat and drink more regularly and he even exercised a little in spite of his limited floor space. He gained weight and was modelling a much healthier shape.

Despite this improvement, as the weeks wore on, both of them were beginning to feel their online chats becoming academic, each conversation seeming like the last. They found the limitations of their phones inhibiting them and they were noticing how impersonal their interactions felt. As time went on, each became nothing but a two dimensional sprite to the other; an avatar trapped in a small rectangle that fit in their palm. The feelings aroused by the train weren't enough any more. Had it *not* been for the train, their online interactions might have sufficed. They would have no pre-notion of the other and could have remained in satisfactory ignorance. But they had, they had known each other differently, and neither could forget. The face they saw on their screen was only a facsimile, it was not the same person they knew from the train.

One evening, they were both sat in silence, they couldn't even bring themselves to look at the other. Jago was staring at the floor, his face forlorn and looking like stone. It was beginning to crystallise that this would be the extent of their relationship. This small copy of her was all that he had; he would never see her completely again. This realisation pained him, the wound only deepening with her just a turn of a head away. He winced and screwed his face together, hoping the pain might be easier to comprehend if he could manifest it physically.

Then he spoke, cutting through the dead silence.

'We can't speak again,' he told her.

She stiffened and tried to tame a wave of emotions from drowning her.

She retraced his steps, trying to understand how he had come to say what he had said; it was so definitive and resolute. Then she walked in those steps, the ones she imagined he must have taken, and then she understood him perfectly. He could no longer see her like this and only like this, it had become too painful to think of what might be.

She cursed her phone for how it separated them, and she damned the city for keeping them apart. Knowing now the firmness of his conviction, her feelings for him only strengthened. He had chosen to believe they might yet be able to forget the other. He had decided they couldn't continue half heartedly and living in torturous hope.

She looked at her screen. He was still looking away.

Three, two, one, zero.

3
A SECRET PLAN

Winter was approaching and all of Jago's maladies had returned. He'd retreated back to his bed where the covers could comfort and hide him. Every early evening, he checked his phone, but no message from her ever came. So he would type one out for her instead, but it would always remain unsent. He could only try to forget her now.

But then, one morning, half awake and unfocused, he heard it, grinding against the bedside table and jarring him to. He felt for his phone and through blurry eyes looked at the screen. He couldn't make it out at first; two identical messages floating around each other. He screwed his eyes up and blinked in a flurry. The messages came together. It was from her.

Have you ever wanted to start over?

Jago at once was perturbed. The words seemed somehow like they didn't belong to her and he had the same foreboding now as when he'd received her very first message.

But now, he felt drawn by something else, something more than curiosity, and something more persuasive than regret: inside him swelled the thrill of insubordination. He couldn't assail it. This message felt different than the others; there was more to her and more to these messages, he was sure of it. Besides, he had nothing else left but this crumb of possibility, this soft resistance.

He replied.

Yes, I think about it a lot.

Ever since she'd met them, she'd been confronted with the consequences of her complicity. The faces she'd once pitied, now haunted her, because now she understood them. They weren't a job any more, they were something real. Sometimes they angered her, to think how docile they were, and how kept, but mostly, she felt guilty for the part she played.

To see the endless misery in them was sapping her. She was tired, not physically, but drained and listless. The group were the only brief spark she had left.

Then she'd seen him, lost just like the rest. She wanted to help him and what she saw on that train car had given her hope. He'd been possessed, at least by enmity, and probably pride. He'd stood up and defied them, and he had bled for his contumacy. Could he be the excuse she needed? Could he be her reason to leave?

The next morning, Jago's phone buzzed several times, nearly falling from the edge of the side table from the vibration. He caught it just as it did and looked at the screen.

There were nine messages from her.

Tomorrow.

Sunrise.

Wait for

Me outside.

Plug phone in.

Leave it in

Your unit. Will

Explain everything.

Are you in...?

He read through it all again...and again — gathering the fragmentation was to throw off the bots.

But what was all this subterfuge, he thought. And in what had he become embroiled? Such espionage did not become him, he hadn't the stomach for it, nor the heart for such dissent.

She must have mistaken him for someone else, these messages were not for him.

He let the phone slip through his hand. It fell onto the covers.

He wanted to stay in his bed and pull the sheets back over him once more, shut out everything and stay there forever. Like a child, he would be safe there, nothing could get him.

He stared at his window and at the glinting light again. He closed his eyes and thought about the concatenation of events that had led him here; his mother, the train, the guard, the message, and now this. A conspiring of circumstance had culminated in a single choice: would he hide in his room or would he go out and meet her?

He found himself paralysed by his indecision, he was faltering. Then he remembered his mother's words; she had wanted him to at least try, try for something more. Could he really live with himself if he failed this test? What had he left to lose?

He was decided. He grabbed his phone from under him, typed his response and sent it.

I'm in.

Now he was at the mercy of her fate.

4
ESCAPE FROM THE CITY

It was just before sunrise and Jago was waiting in the lobby under the stairwell, watching the entrance for the light of any approaching vehicles. He had been there a while when finally a light did appear, pouring through the gaps in the boarding and running along the ceiling and onto the walls. Then the light went off, then on, then off again once more. It must have been a signal. Jago tried not to think about what he was doing. He crept from the lobby and went outside. He couldn't make anything out in the darkness of the street so he moved closer to where the light had come from. He saw the vague outline of a car and went to it. He could see on the side of it, the word SAFETY embossed across the panel, KEEPING YOU SAFE just below. Jago's heart leapt as it warned him away. He doubted himself but pushed forward; he couldn't turn back now. Through the tinted window at the front, he noticed a shadow moving around inside, then something homologous seeming to point to the passenger seat. He looked and noticed the back door ajar. He got in, the door closed behind him. He turned, four walls surrounded him and closed him in. He couldn't see outside or through to the front seat. He felt trapped. He tried the door but it was locked now. The car had ensnared him. What had he done, he thought, how could he be so stupid? Then a panel slid open in front of him. Jago braced. An arm appeared. Then hair also. Then a pair of familiar eyes were looking back at him. It was her.

They looked at each other, this time through their own eyes, and were lost for a moment.

'It's me,' she said.

'Yes, I figured,' Jago quipped in a rush of relief.

She almost laughed at the inanity.

'So now you know about me,' she continued, 'Well, at least some of it, I will explain more on the way, but now we need to leave.'

She leant towards him.

'But first, I have an important question.' She sounded rehearsed. Jago was absorbed. 'We're going to leave the city, for good. If you come, that's it, you can't return to your unit, you can't return to your life here. Everything will be different from now on. So, I guess my question is again...'

She took a breath.

'Are you in?'

Jago's face was blank, he was still trying to process what was happening. He noticed a flash of worry run over her face as he was yet to answer. Then he glanced up in the direction of his room, but only the inside of the car looked back. He realised there was nothing worth seeing up there anyway.

'You can go back now,' she added, 'They'll never know—'

'Okay,' he answered, interrupting her, 'Let's go.'

An odd calmness had come over him.

She nodded, turning back to the front.

The car sped away, pushing Jago into his seat. The lights came back on again and the car slowed as she started to drive steadily through the streets. Jago wondered why at first, then realised it was so they wouldn't attract attention.

'You know what I am now then,' she said after a while, 'You'd probably say, *I'm one of them*.'

She glanced at the rear mirror and through the panel at him. There was no reaction.

'Aren't you surprised?' she asked.

Jago looked back at her, blank faced.

'No, actually,' he replied, 'nothing would really surprise me about you at this point.'

She smirked.

'You left your phone in your unit, right?' she checked.

'Yes.'

'Plugged in?'

'Yes. They'll think I'm still in there, I suppose?' he guessed.

'Exactly.'

'And won't they notice me gone?' he asked

'Who?'

'Your lot, you know, safeties, guards...?'

She paused for a moment.

'You really don't have a clue, do you?,' she said, 'There's no one checking up on you, how could we possibly check up on everyone, we barely even do searches any more. No, it's all the other stuff that does our job for us: the notices, the signs, the messages, the news, social media…and…well, you know, you do too, you civis; you police each other. We don't have to do much at all really.' She glanced at him in the mirror again. 'See…it's all coming together, right?'

Jago looked pensively back at her, then away again.

They drove for a while in silence as Jago tried to untangle what she'd said. She occasionally looked back at him and saw him vacantly staring at the window.

She let him in peace for a while.

'You never asked why.'

'What?' Jago responded, as her words brought him to.

'You never asked why I'm doing this,' she repeated.

Jago looked at her in the mirror.

'I was drafted to the safeties a few years ago,' she began, 'I got all the training, all the programming and I did what I was told. I was like them for a long time, I didn't really think anything of it, it was my job and I thought I had to be like that to keep order and to keep everyone safe. I thought that was the best thing for the city and everyone in it.'

She checked from side to side as she slowed to a junction.

'But something changed,' she continued, 'I met some people, they were quietly resisting, I guess. They wanted just a modicum of a normal life again. But it was so hard for them, they could be caught at any moment. That was *our* fault, I started to see that, I started to see the impact we were having on people's lives…we weren't helping them at all, we were throttling them.'

She pulled away then glanced at him again.

'I feel like this is more of a sit down kind of conversation, but anyway…,' she said, though she actually found she preferred not having to look at him for this, 'I couldn't keep doing it, working for the city, seeing the damage we were doing, day in, day out. It was too much, I had to get out, somehow, leave… But I couldn't quite bring myself to do it, I needed some catalyst…

And... I don't want to flatter your ego too much but I thought, maybe that was you. When I saw you on the train, I was...intrigued, let's say. Then all that stuff happened. I hadn't expected you to do that at all - no offence! - and I thought, maybe this guy's a bit different. Most of them like to pretend everything's okay, they don't even want to be helped, but, I thought, maybe you did. So I took a gamble on you...and...well, here we are.'

Jago thought for a moment.

'...So...that's why the safety on the train ignored you,' he said, 'It knew you, I suppose...?'

'Yes,' she replied.

'And, you couldn't react in front of it...?'

'Something like that, I couldn't help you either of course, not there. After the guard scanned you and left, I couldn't just stay, it would've looked suspicious.'

'...And...but...why were you not in uniform? You were in civi clothing...'

'Yes, I was off duty. I had finished my shift.'

For now, Jago's catechising came to an end.

They passed several more junctions. No other cars were around.

'By the way,' she said, seeing a road sign coming up, 'If we get stopped, just stay quiet, I'm taking you to a correction cell.'

Jago looked doubtful.

'That'll work?' he questioned.

'Why not? You have a better idea?'

'Well, no, but I haven't been thinking of one like you have.'

She smirked.

'So what exactly am I being corrected for then?' he asked.

She smiled impudently.

'Not having your phone with you of course,' she said, with a knowing glance.

'Makes sense,' he muttered, somewhat approving.

Jago watched through the open panel as the empty streets went by, still in deep negotiation with his thoughts. It all seemed so preposterous that he had no choice but to treat the situation with detachment and divorce. He was only a thin reality away from hysteria.

'So where is everyone?' he said.

'*Everyone?*' she replied, 'They're all inside."

'But...where's all the fighting? Where-where's all the traitors?' Jago started to stutter, 'The-the streets are all empty...'

'Yes, they're always empty,' she said calmly.

'But...I-I thought there was supposed to be fighting, it-it was supposed to be dangerous outside...'

She could hear the despairing in his voice and looked back at him with sympathy, the tumult was getting the better of him.

'There's no fighting,' she said softly. There was no response. 'It might take a while for this all to sink in...but, but just give it time.'

Jago sat bolt upright and looked pleadingly into the mirror.

'But-but why is everything boarded up if there's no danger...? It's to protect us, right? It's-it's got to be!'

She sighed seeing the morass he was in.

'The boarding's not to keep you safe,' she said, 'it's to stop you from seeing.'

His expression didn't changed.

'Look, it's two things,' she explained, 'if you can't see then you don't know what's going on, right? It stops you from seeing what's actually happening. Second, if you can see outside, then you might want to *go* outside. And they don't want you getting any silly ideas like that. They'd rather you go online to see a sunset, not actually go outside and look at one.'

Jago sat back in his seat slowly.

He breathed in deeply and mouthed the words, '*Lies trap...*'

'Huh?' she said.

He didn't explain.

'What about the announcements then?' he asked instead.

'*Announcements?*' she responded.

'On the train, the announcement telling us to keep apart?'

'Ah,' she said, 'that kind of stuff is designed to separate people, stop people interacting with each other. There's loads of that kind of messaging everywhere, it's very important to stop people getting together and actually talking. Well, we couldn't have that, could we? I mean, look what happened with us, look where we are now, all because we happened to sit *too close* on a train. And we didn't even say one word to each other. That's the power of company, I suppose.'

She watched him turn back to the window and that glazed over look returned. His body became deathly still, but she knew it betrayed a desperate longing for balance within. His enlightenment was taking its toll and she could almost feel the dawning realisation in him. He was having to re-contextualise everything in his life all at once, the whole artifice was crumbling.

She saw another road sign approaching.

'I need to close this now,' she said, indicating the panel between them, 'There's more likely to be patrols in this next district.'

'Wait, one more thing,' he said hastily, remembering something important, 'What about the perimeter though? How do we get passed *that*?'

'*The perimeter*?' she said airily, then with confidence she added, 'You don't need to worry about the perimeter.'

Jago thought he caught another knowing glance from her and she slid the panel shut between them.

5
THE PERIMETER

Rain descended. Jago heard it scatter on the roof then become a deafening deluge. He suddenly felt distant from her, his senses dulled from the noise. Then the panel opened again and he heard the faintest of shouts from her over the storm.

'See, it's a blessing! Even safeties don't want to be caught in the rain!'

She was right, the streets remained bare. The torrent seemed to be the equaliser, no one, not even the guards, wanted to be out in it.

The car battled through the rain and the wind then gradually, the storm softened and passed. And the night, that too passed as the early morning light began to clear it and lift the sky. Jago watched through the open panel as daytime arrived, and with it, he felt his uncertainty effaced; the light would now protect them. The city started to fragment, in its place came the neglected suburbia indicative of the outskirts. Then this too passed as they came out over large spates of unoccupied land. Only dirt stretched out before them. The land was barren.

Jago estimated that they must nearly be at the city limits.

'We must be coming up to the perimeter soon...,' he said curiously.

'Mm, yes, must be,' she responded.

He sensed sarcasm.

'So...what's your plan?' he persisted.

She didn't reply, only raising her eyebrows at him. He looked away again in thought.

Jago considered everything she'd spoken of throughout their journey. He thought about the boarded up windows and how they stopped him from seeing what was outside. He thought about all the rules, and all the signs that reinforced them; they were ubiquitous, pervasive, unavoidable. He thought about the guards; the impracticality of their uniforms and their masks and their shields; what purpose had they but for useful intimidation? Then he thought finally of the perimeter; that impenetrable, unbreakable barrier he'd always been told about.

Fear controls, he thought.

Then he surmised.

'There is no perimeter, is there...'

Jago looked up at the mirror again and saw her glad face looking back.

'No,' she said, 'no, there's not.'

6
INTRODUCTIONS

The landscape continued to alter through the frame of the open panel between them; the urbane displaced by the great gamut of nature. Jago could make out hills ahead of him, verdant fields each side, with trees aligning them and hedgerows segmenting them. Even in the gloom of dawn, his small window to the outside was an ever adapting canvas, vivid and colourful and dynamic. He felt the air change auspiciously, even from his snug in the back — she had opened a window — and a redolent freshness invigorated him. He closed his eyes and felt the breeze run through the hairs on his skin.

'We'll have to stop soon,' came a voice from the front again, 'We're running out of power.'

Jago opened his eyes.

'Where were you planning to go?' he said.

'As far away as possible.'

They came off the track and entered a wooded area.

'Don't want any drones seeing the car,' she mentioned nonchalantly.

'*Drones?*' Jago repeated, wanting some clarification. None was received.

The car began to slow, its power drained, and it rolled gradually to a stop.

Jago tried the door and it opened this time. He got out of the cramped back seat and was hit by an onrush of strong, virulent air. He breathed it in, that and *all* the qualia of the countryside, trying to inhale as much of it as he could. Then he took a step, but his knee buckled, his cramped leg too weak to support him. He leant back against the car for support and tried to shake the blood back to his legs.

She joined him from the driver's compartment, having changed from her uniform.

'All good?' she said, seeing him in difficulty.

'Yes.' Then he nodded towards her feet, 'Blue trainers.'

'Yes, just for you.'

She half smiled and walked round to the boot of the car, opened it and took out two large bags.

Jago took a couple of steps gingerly towards her.

'What's in there?' he said.

'Water, supplies, tools, anything we need really.'

Jago paused and looked around his new organic surroundings.

'Have you been here before?' he asked.

'No, not this far, I've only come just beyond the outskirts.' She put one bag on the ground and took the other to him. 'I don't know any more than you do now,' she added as she handed him the bag.

Jago was so enchanted by the woods, he hardly noticed the weight of the bag rest on his shoulder; he'd been estranged from nature's kind of design and colour for so long.

'It's amazing, isn't it,' she said, standing just beside him.

He nodded.

They stood for a brief moment, staring out into the woods. Then she put her hand on his shoulder.

'We need to get as much distance as we can between us and the car,' she said, 'Can you walk okay?'

'Yes, I'll be fine,' he replied.

She took the other bag from the ground and they started walking through the woods, leaving the car behind.

They'd walked for a while, looking at each other every so often and smiling in appreciation of their new and remarkable circumstances. They would look above them and see patches of sky and cloud scrolling between the tree tops. They would touch the rough bark on the trees interestedly and moss stained their hands. And the uneven and treacherous earth below them, with it's fallen branches, vines and damp soil, would educate their sheltered feet. It was surreal, unimaginable, unreal, and they wondered how they could have possibly come this far. What a weird world they now found themselves.

'Did you think you'd end up here when you woke up today?' she asked him.

'No...well, I didn't sleep much last night anyhow,' Jago responded, 'So have you ever seen anything like it?'

'No, nothing like this, I always lived in the city. How about you?'

'Yes, when I was child, I lived in the country, but I don't remember much.'

'You were moved with the others then?'

'Yes, we didn't have a choice.'

'No, 'course...'

The trees thinned and the sky opened out above them. They walked a little further, then breaked for some food, finding an area of flat grass to sit down on. There was a short silence imposed by their eating, then Jago spoke first.

'So how did you find me then...?' he queried, 'I mean, you only saw me, right, on the train? You couldn't have known who I was.'

She chewed the last of her packed ration. 'I scanned your phone,' she explained, 'when the other safety was there, got your ID.'

'...and then you could locate my unit...'

'Exactly.' She gave him a look. 'You're getting pretty savvy on all this now.'

Jago opened his mouth as if to speak but then didn't. He had wanted to tell her something since they'd left the city. He mouthed the words a few times, then spoke them finally.

'Thank you...,' he said, 'for all of this.'

As he heard them, the words sounded dryer and less sincere than he'd hoped. She smiled anyway, interpreting his gesture with the gravity with which it was intended.

'Sure, no problem,' she said.

After lunching, they wandered on. They trekked through the dirt, snapping twigs underfoot and scuffing up moribund leaves. The woodland then became thick with dewily vines and they had to pull them aside to pass. Once they were clear, Jago was first to break the silence once again.

'So you go up and down trains looking for people you might like?'

He had asked this so straight faced and so out-of-the-blue that it took her a moment to realise he was joking.

'Mm...yes...something like that,' she said chuckling, 'No, I said before, I'd finished my shift. I go home on the train.'

'But why?' he questioned, 'There's so few of them now and...you have a car...'

'No I don't,' she answered, 'The cars stay at the safety house. I took this one out first thing, there's hardly anyone around then.'

Jago thought about this.

'...And...but don't they track them?'

'Sometimes. But it's dead now, isn't it? So no more signal.'

She looked at him.

He looked back expectantly.

'You know,' she said, 'I didn't know what would happen. I was just intrigued. I didn't think another safety would come passed.'

'Not your fault, I didn't have to do what I did... I don't know what came over me, I really don't. I was just so annoyed at it —'

' — *for ruining our moment*...?' she jumped in, ribbing him with a voice of mock erudition.

'Exactly, *how rude of it*,' he added, playing along with a silly voice of his own.

They laughed, settling down after a moment.

'So what do you think would have happened if the guard hadn't have come?' she said wondering.

'I don't know, probably nothing,' he replied, 'I suppose I can thank it for goading me, you wouldn't have contacted me otherwise, and without that fight, I certainly wouldn't have replied even if you did.'

The autumn day had already started to darken as they came out from the woods. They couldn't see far but they were walking now over open fields and the wind set upon them brutishly. They could feel the cold deep in their bones and their breath was short and gasping.

'We'll need shelter soon,' Jago shouted over the rough wind.

She nodded. They both shivered.

Jago was tired, he wasn't used to walking but he didn't want to tell her. He slowed considerably, unable to drag the legs beneath him.

Soon they came across what they were sure was a farm and they hoped there might be a roof somewhere nearby to sleep under. The night drew in rapidly and they could barely see anything. But a structure finally came into view and they hobbled over to it, desperate to be out of the abrasive wind. They leant on each other for support, moving as one fumbling mass. There were two smaller buildings, then a barn between them and they hurried inside it, seeing bales they could lie on. They pulled the doors to behind them and were relieved to be rid of the harsh outdoors. They collapsed onto the bales, then she took out blankets from one of the bags to warm them.

'At least it's not full blown winter quite yet,' she said as she put the blankets over them.

'Feels like it though,' Jago responded, feeling the draft coming through gaps in the ramshackle walls, 'I think it will be a cold one this year.'

They both lay back exhausted, they could barely muster any more words between them.

As she rested, it occurred to her there was something she didn't know about him, far more personal than his identity number. She wondered how it could have been that it had never come up, perhaps formalities were something foreign to them now. Her eyes closed and she whispered.

'What's your name?'

With his last sleepy effort, he mumbled, 'Jago...and yours?'

Jago, she thought, that's a nice name.

She whispered again, even more softly.

'Amica.'

Moments later, they were both asleep.

7
WATER AND FIRE

When he woke, morning was waiting for them outside the barn. He looked over at Amica, who was still resting. He rose quietly off the bales and went to the door, opening it slowly as not to disturb her. He left the barn, wanting to see the surroundings in the daytime. He came outside. He could still feel the cold but now, the moody and miserable terrain from the night before, had transformed. Light streamed down onto the same fields, the same trees, the same barn, but now a heliacal brush had painted them their auburn palette. On each side the dense thickets bordered the long strokes of the fields, stretching into the distance. Jago's feet had shuffled through more fallen leaves, which masked most of the dirt track underneath. But he recalled the path they'd entered; the signs of the leaf and mud displacement they'd caused still visible. The path forked at the barn, one track led across the fields, and the other downwards, disappearing into more woods.

Jago went to take another step, but a voice stopped him.

'Leaving already?' it said.

Jago turned around.

'Yes, I've already had enough,' he said po-faced.

Amica, more versed in his humour now, brushed it off. She walked over to the fence to the side of the barn and sat between the rails.

'Sleep well?' she asked him.

'Yes,' Jago replied, walking over and perching down next to her, 'And you?'

'Not sure I've slept better actually.'

They shivered again from the cold, but it wasn't enough to persuade them to go back inside.

'It must be hard for a safety to just get up and leave like that?' Jago pondered.

'What are they going to do? I'm not there any more, am I?' responded Amica.

'But what about out here? Will they come after you *here*?'

'Maybe.'

'*Maybe*?'

'Yes, we sometimes use drones to search for people, they might send one.'

'Like the delivery drones?' Jago sounded shocked.

'Yes,' she answered, 'They're not too bothered about civis, but me...I know them, know some of their secrets. It's not good for them me being around.'

Jago frowned. She noticed it.

'But probably not,' she added, 'it's a massive drain on resources sending anything out of the city.'

The wind picked up and interrupted them. They listened to it whistle through the trees and scatter the leaves. She turned to face him.

'What?' he asked.

She blinked slowly, seeming to take in the serenity.

'It's just nice not to have a countdown,' she said.

Amica stood up from the fence and studied the fork in the pathway.

'We should find water soon,' she suggested, 'I couldn't bring much with me, it would've weighed the car down, drained the power.'

Jago nodded to one of the tracks.

'Well, that way leads down,' he said, 'We should go that way.'

'Sounds like a plan,' Amica agreed, 'I'll get the bags.'

They had wandered for most of the day, feeling refreshed by their sleep and buoyed by the nature around them. They walked wistfully, unencumbered, just enjoying the companionship of the other. And as if their positivity manifested it, their path from the woods opened out to the sight of a large body of water off in the distance. They hiked towards it, eventually coming out to the foot of a river. They dropped their bags a way off, the containers for the water in them clunking down. They shared a glance, then broke out into a jog to the water's edge and splashed a few strides into it. Jago knelt down and threw water over his face, the cold of it shocked his skin.

'Do you think it's clean?' Amica said, standing just beside him.

'We can treat it. You have something to start a fire in that bag of yours, I presume?'

'Of course. Let's fill 'em up, and take them back.'

They filled up the depleted containers with the river water and packed them back into the bags. Then, taking a moment, they washed themselves. Amica had even brought with her a bar of soap stashed from the city, which they used liberally. Jago hadn't been allowed soap for many years, it was a luxury item, and the smell of it was overpowering for him. They both came away from the water feeling cleansed after their tiring and tense journey.

After their lavation, they slung their bags, now replete with supplies of water, onto their backs and left to return to the farm.

Night was shortly arriving, the temperature dropping. They cleared an area outside the barn of leaves, found wood from the two outbuildings and arranged a fire. Amica took fire lighters and a box of matches from her miscellaneous tool bag. The wind would intervene on two attempts, but on the third, the fire was lit. They sat together for a while, entranced by the flames as they rose, crackled and danced in front of them. The fire burned fiercely and raucously and imparted on them a sensation Amica had never known before and Jago could barely remember.

'You know, I've never even seen fire before, not in real life,' mentioned Amica.

'Really?' Jago responded, 'Well, enjoy it.'

Jago stared into the flames.

Sitting there in the warmth, he realised he no longer felt scared. He was not sure what possessed him to say what he said next, perhaps it was the mood that imbued his lucidity, or maybe he just wanted to unburden himself.

He whispered, barely audibly, 'My mother died,' and the words disappeared with the smoke and silence reigned.

Amica turned to him, placing a consoling hand on his. She wasn't sure how to respond, she felt she wasn't qualified to navigate such emotional territory. But nevertheless, she accepted what she thought was an offering from him. It wasn't a secret he had shared so much, but it was a meaningful event that had shaped him. It was his grief and his most delicate and vulnerable feeling. He had chosen *her* to share it with. She was touched and felt honoured.

'That's why I came with you,' he continued, still staring into the fire, 'She had just died before you messaged. She was all I had left. So there was nothing keeping me there any more.'

She squeezed his hand tighter.

'After she died,' he went on, 'I felt I wanted to die myself. I couldn't keep living, not like that, not stuck inside, doing nothing, with nothing to look forward to. So I just wasted away, just waiting to die, I suppose.'

He kicked some stones into the fire. A wisp of flame flicked up.

'You're not living, you're just existing…,' he quoted, 'That's what she used to say to me. And she was right. It wasn't living, none of it felt real, it was just soulless…empty…'

Jago paused, then picked up a handful of stones from the ground. 'Not like this…,' he said, letting them fall through his fingers, '*This*…, this is real…'

Then he put his hand to the fire and felt the heat, '…and *this*…,' he said, 'this is real…'

Then he turned to her, took her other hand in his, and they stared at each other for a moment.

'And this…,' he whispered, '…*this* is real.'

Amica's eyes teared over. She gripped both his hands.

'I was right about you,' she breathed.

Then she leaned in and kissed him.

Neither moved for a moment. They felt each other's lips on theirs. Then they came apart, only enough so the light from the fire outlined them.

A tear rolled down her cheek.

The fire shaded both their faces and they could see the flames flicker in the others' eyes.

'*Right about me*?' asked Jago.

'Yes,' she said, 'You stood up.'

The two embraced and the fire faded into the night, gradually burning down to its last embers.

8
ENCOUNTER ON THE FARM

Jago and Amica woke hearing voices outside the barn. Discombobulated, they looked around. The strands of first light coming through the walls blinked as shadows flashed across them. They looked at each other and Amica held a finger up to her mouth for them to keep quiet. They remained still for a moment, then Jago pointed towards a gap in the wall and crawled towards it. Amica looked expectantly back at the barn door, willing it to stay shut. Jago peaked through the gap he had found. He could see blurred figures walking around outside. But they weren't guards, and his foremost fears were allayed. Amica crawled up next to him and said in his ear.

'What is it?'

'I think they're okay, they're not safeties,' he replied, then turned to her, 'We should go out.'

Amica was surprised *he* would suggest this so readily, though she was in agreement.

They started to their feet but then, the doors burst open, crashing against the inside of the barn walls. Two figures bustled through, stopping suddenly as they saw them. All four of them stood still, no one was quite sure what to do.

'In here,' one of them called out loudly after a few moments.

More of them appeared from behind.

'Who are you?' the person at the front said.

'We just got here,' Amica said.

Their group looked around at each other, seeming to confer telepathically.

'We escaped the city,' one of them said.

'We saw your smoke in the distance,' another one said.

'We weren't sure if you'd left,' the first one said again.

'Well...we're still here.' Jago observed, somewhat facetiously.

'Yes, we can see that,' the same one at the front countered.

This banter seemed to release the tension and both sides visibly loosened.

'You have water?' the other one at the front asked, after everyone had somewhat relaxed.

'Yes,' replied Amica.

'Okay, well there's a whole river back —'

'We found it, yes,' Amica interrupted her.

'Right,' came a clipped response.

They all waited again for someone else to speak.

'So...,' came a voice from the back, 'What do we do now?'

'Well,' Amica began, glancing at Jago, 'You want to stay here? There's room.'

The group all looked around at each other again.

'What do you reckon, Hy?' the first one asked the one next to him.

'Looks warm,' came a contribution from behind them.

A few more moments passed, then the one who was asked the question spoke again.

'Okay,' she said, 'if you insist.'

4
FIRST CHILD

1
ENDURING THE WINTER

The small community settled in the farm near the woods and by the fields. They had appropriated the barn and the two outbuildings there to reside. But a harsh winter set upon them sharply as autumn ended and the group had no choice but to stay in the barn to keep warm. They found they couldn't venture far in the cold before they started to freeze. They would have to endure the season inside with what limited supplies they already had and wait for the more hospitable weather of spring to gather more resources.

Soon, their supplies and what little they could reap from the immediate area were not enough to sustain them. They became weak and this precipitated the spread of disease from their squalor. Confounded by their weak immunity from their isolation in the city, they had no intolerance and were acutely vulnerable to even the mildest of viruses. So it was only the common cold that seized them. It incapacitated them and bound them to their beds.

Only the two eldest members of the group, Ophelia and Caius, were able to provide some support for the others. They had lived a lifetime before the city, experiencing all kinds of illness, and their insusceptibility kept them in more workable health. The two of them would cover the group in blankets, feed them each day and give them water. They even lit small fires in the barn when they could, with what materials they could find.

Eventually, it was the cold itself that did for Caius and Ophelia. Having forgoed their own share of the food supplies for the benefit of the others, they had no energy left and their frailness left them defenceless against their environment. They began to deteriorate.

Ophelia died. Her body froze, simply giving up amid the harshness pervading it. Caius had lost a close friend and his only ally in looking after the others. They had lain next to each other in the barn and one night Caius had spoken to her and there was no response. She was cold and still. Caius carried her body out to the woods to bury her, he hadn't wanted the others to see her lifeless like that. But out in the unbearable cold, he had no strength left to dig and though he tried, he just collapsed next to her. Caius died too. They were left lying next to each other in the woods, just how they had in the barn.

The group was now at its lowest ebb. The winter was far from relenting. A few of them in their delirium, even considered making for the city, and back to their rooms. But they were convinced otherwise by the others, told they would certainly die on the way back. They almost hadn't noticed the disappearance of Ophelia and Caius through their tribulation but soon their footprints were discovered leading to the woods. The loss immured the group in grief and they lay disconsolate and cadaverous and with little hope amongst them.

But something miraculous happened.

Three dogs had come to the farm to investigate the new smell of burning, thinking there might be food. They moped around the field and explored the outbuildings. Then they wandered right into the barn, squeezing through the gaps in the walls. Some of the group had never seen a dog before, so when they were nuzzled awake by them, they thought they might be hallucinating. The dogs foraged through the hay in the barn and everyone, now sat up from their beds, watched in disbelief. The dogs were painfully malnourished, emaciated, and they were pining for food. The group were instantly rallied by their empathy for them, which came rushing to the fore. Giving up their own dwindling rations, they fed, watered and looked after them.

It was in this care for the dogs that the group found cause to remain cognisant. The dogs hung around and the group would pet them and they would respond with affection in kind. It was Hya who pointed out cynically that they were only interested in the remaining food but the rest quickly shot her down, maintaining it was the camaraderie that kept them there.

Their arrival also coincided with the seasonal change and so with the cold gradually abating, the group started to improve, the warmer temperatures easing some of their symptoms.

Though they were still desperately hungry, they were no longer so debilitated. They were now able to travel further to find food, even having enough strength to fish in the river. The dogs also returned the group's initial favour as they were particularly practised in foraging. They continued to stay with them; they slept when they slept, and went where they went, fast becoming honorary members of the team.

When it came to naming them, a debate reared that became unduly fractious. Some of the group were quite possessive of certain dogs and were attached to names they'd already given them. It was a contentious issue for them but also served as a helpful distraction from their subsistence. Both Otto and Ever had taken a shining to the middle sized dog; one wanted to name him Spot, and the other, Chaser. An argument between them escalated to shoving and the others had to come between them. For the sake of fairness, neither Spot nor Chaser would be up for consideration. The others were actually glad of this excuse to discard these names, as no one else liked them anyway, thinking they were too stereotypical. This rare melodrama had the added bonus of amping up the group too, none of them having felt these kinds of primal emotions since their escape. They were beginning to feel more human again.

After much deliberation, they would eventually agree on the names, Rogue, Arrow and Calix, for the larger, medium and smaller dog respectively. And with this, the three canines had now officially joined the group. On their naming day, they were taken down to the river and were washed for the first time. The group were thorough, seeing that all manner of strife had messed the dogs before they had come to the farm. As much as they protested and whined, they were submerged in the water, and every blade of fur on them was scrubbed diligently. Annia joked that this was a kind of baptism for them.

The group were rather surprised that the dogs had even stayed with them. They'd presumed they must have degenerated over years in the wild and become rabid, but somehow, they were able to assimilate nicely. Once shivering, withered and leaden, they were now plump, playful and exuberant. The group's initial sacrificing of their *own* food, now seemed worthwhile.

Symbiotically, the humans became healthier too. They were finally starting to adapt to the rigours of the outdoors. They farmed on the arable land around them, fished regularly and explored the local area for edible fruits and vegetables. Their plight was cyclical; the more food they had, the stronger they were and the more food they could grow or gather. As spring came, they were beginning to enjoy a salubrious way of life.

Spring too would pass and they were now in the heart of summer. The group, encouraged by the warmth and the sunshine, would walk over the fields, through the woods and by the river, happily appreciating their new eudaimonia. But with the smoother running of the daily upkeep demanding less of their time, they soon looked for other recreation.

Draven, with experience in carpentry, had already created for them a few basic tables and chairs, and even some rudimentary crockery and cutlery. So as an aside, he set about making a ball that the group could throw for the dogs. He stretched some cloth they had found and packed it tightly with hay. Once he had patched up the cloth into a roughly circular shape, it was put to the test with the dogs. They promptly tore it apart. Draven started again, refining the stitching and made a second ball. This time it remained in tact for longer, was of better make and less oblate.

Though they enjoyed playing fetch with the dogs, the group soon took the ball for themselves and would begin to play catch with it or kick it about. A game was quickly established where by each would take turns to kick the ball at the side of the barn. If they couldn't hit the wall from their position, they would lose a point, and if they lost three points, they would be out of the game. This became known as barn football.

The law of the city had perforce meant that no such games could be played, so even this simple sport excited energies which were exhilarating for the group. Jago, who had been implementary with the games, at once was reminded of his childhood, where he would play football in the fields with his friends. With his new rural sodality, he felt the same energy and the same togetherness he had felt back then. He couldn't believe these were the same people, bed ridden over the winter, who now shuttled about after a ball in the bright lights of the summer. The group was buoyant and the community was thriving.

2
DRONE

The first signs of the following autumn had brushed over the land. A florid tinge had pattinated the landscape and the leafs had started to collect at the bases of trees again. Amica was pregnant. And when her resulting prominent physicality had manifested for the group to see, they were overjoyed. Most of them had never seen a baby before and couldn't wait for its arrival. Amica and Jago had decided on the name Cato for a boy and Djuna for a girl. They had recognised in their own names, Jago and Amica, the enunciated vowel sound ending, and so wanted to continue this through the appellation of their children. A number of favourites were then whittled down to these two options and a short time later, Cato was born.

The group adored him and they basked Cato with attention. He was passed around the group like a new toy to play with and nearly everyone wanted to hold him. They hadn't seen such tiny and fragile features before and were enamoured. Cato didn't seem objectionable to any of them coddling him. He heard so many voices and felt the warmth of so many hands, and was immersed readily into the bosom of the group.

Hya however, was the exception, she stayed distant from him and couldn't understand the fascination and the hype. She found the baby uninteresting and was perturbed by his indiscriminate noise. With this, Jago and Amica thought it best to move into one of the outbuildings on the farm where Cato couldn't disturb her, or any of the others, from sleeping. The three of them quickly made a comfy and more private home for themselves there.

With Jago and Amica as the exemplar, the group had naturally started to couple up. The seeds of interest had been germinating even as far back as the subway and in the case of Hya and Rumer, as far back as the fire alarm itself; the first time they'd met. The winter had postponed most socialising between the group, then so too did the hard work establishing the settlement over the spring, but now through the summer, relationships were free to develop.

Rumer and Hya had become very close. There was chemistry between them even during their brief interaction outside their building. This then flowered through their epistolic communication. With all physicality suspended during this time, they only became more desirous of the other and when they were finally able to meet again, this propelled them into their union.

Hya had also opened up to Rumer about her unique attachment to Caius; that he had reminded her of her own father. When Caius had died, old grief had been dredged up for her. She'd kept this hidden from all but Rumer, who felt privileged to be confided in, especially given Hya's usual reservedness.

Rumer also liked to help look after Cato, the baby, as much as she could. She was completely besotted by him. But even after seeing Rumer's affection for him, Hya's opinion of children had not softened.

Then there was Ever and Cleo. They had also had a short private letter exchange back in the city, then had continued talking in the underground and had hardly stopped since. They were the only couple to feel they needed to call a meeting of the group to announce their officialdom. They had done so very excitedly but the others weren't entirely sure why such a formality was necessary; afterwards, they'd all trundled off, feeling rather inconvenienced.

And lastly, there was Annia and Otto. Despite their best efforts at surreptitiousness, it was patently obvious to everyone, they were something of an item. The two of them seemed to be joined at the hip, and wherever one was, the other wouldn't be far behind. But whenever anyone hinted to them at the possibility of a romance, they insisted they were merely good friends.

Then there was Draven: the extra cog and the mathematical odd one out. He was older, in his mid forties and with the absence of Caius and Ophelia, he already felt his age separated him from the others, their partnering up only alienating him further.

Because of this, he'd elected to take the second outbuilding to live in; it was somewhere he could be on his own. He'd always been reclusive, only ever interacting with the group minimally, and living apart from them closeted him away. He spent most of his time on his lonesome and when he wasn't constructing things for the group, he enjoyed long hikes into the heart of the countryside. There, he could find tranquillity away from the camp. The others wanted to assume he was quite content on his own, but they still worried for him and wished he would involve himself more socially.

On one of his outings, Draven had hiked a few hours from the farm and was wiling away an afternoon lying on a declivity of grassland on the moors. He enjoyed it there, it was a favourite spot of his. There was a vista of hills in the distance and the grass he lay on was plush. His hands interlocked behind his head, propping him up so he could see the views. The sun was baying over him and he was still hot from walking, sweat had matted his shirt to his body. He made a note to stop and bathe in the river on his way home.

He released his hands and let his head fall back onto the thick grass. He watched the clouds, with their cartoonish contours, as they raced across the sky. He remembered there *was* no sky back in the city, only a dark haze above and buildings that blocked the view. He felt blessed to be where he was.

He planned to lie there until the sun had gone and the cold evicted him. He closed his eyes for a while and felt the tickling of the grass on the back of his ears.

He heard a distant hum. It sounded unnatural, mechanical. It grew louder and closer. He opened his eyes but couldn't see the source of it. He got to his feet and paced over cautiously to the long grass, finding cover. He lay on his front and peered up through the grass. Then he noticed something in the sky a distance away and retreated further into the vegetation carefully. He kept his eyes poised on the flying object. It then stopped and hovered. Draven tightened up, thinking it must have seen him. He kept as still as he could. It twitched, rotated left, then right, then left again. Then it flew on, vanishing behind the clouds.

Draven could feel his heart thumping against the ground. He waited prudently until the cover of the night sky, then got back to his feet and started back for the farm. Finding his way by rote in the dark, he went as quickly as he could. He needed to tell the others.

'Draven, where have you been?' enquired Annia, part of a small contingent outside the barn when he returned.

'Are you setting a fire tonight?' Draven said, breathlessly.

'No, it's too warm this evening,' answered Annia.

'Good, no more fires for a while,' he said, 'I have to tell you all something. Where is everyone?'

'In the barn,' Hya replied, also with them.

'Okay, let's talk inside,' gasped Draven. He entered the barn and motioned for the others to follow.

Hya, Rumer and Annia saw the dirt over his chest and knees, and the sweat stains on his top. They didn't correlate with the cooler evening air and they were concerned for him.

'Are you okay?' Annia asked as they went into the barn.

'Yes, fine. Everybody...,' the last word Draven spoke loudly, addressing the whole group. Inside already were Amica; rocking Cato, Jago, Otto, Ever and Cleo. '...I saw a drone,' Draven announced.

'A *drone*?' Amica said, not raising her voice for the sake of the baby, 'How near?'

Though the group were unaware, Amica immediately thought the drone had been sent for her. She shrewdly kept this to herself, at least for now, and she trusted Jago, who would likely figure this too, to do the same.

'A few hours hike from here, on the moors,' Draven replied.

'The same ones they use in the city?' Otto jumped in, '...To deliver stuff?'

'Yes probably, it looked the same.'

'What could it have been doing so far out...?' Annia mused, thinking aloud.

'Looking for us maybe,' added Hya.

'It wouldn't care much about us, right?' said Ever, looking around for assurance from anyone who might offer it.

'They would if people found out someone escaped,' said Annia.

'How would anyone find out?' Otto argued, 'You know what they're like, they'll have removed all trace of us in no time. And they'll be no news of it of course.'

'Maybe, but I know for sure they don't want people outside the city. Why move them all in in the first place?' Annia contested.

'Oh, come on. That's one drone in nearly a year. I think you're overreacting.'

There was a gap in the discussion.

'So what should we do?' said Ever, restarting it.

Amica, still with Cato in her arms, spoke up, quietly again.

'You're half right,' she said, 'They don't care about you, but they do sometimes search outside the city.'

'How do *you* know?' Otto challenged.

'I just know,' she responded, glancing at Jago furtively enough so only he would notice. 'There's nothing else we can do, we just have to stay low for a while. No more outdoor fires, we can have them supervised in here if we need to.'

'And keep your eyes out for anything when you're outside,' included Hya, 'Report back if you see anything.'

Draven nodded. He was satisfied with the outcome and tempered by the thought of the infrequency with which the drone had appeared.

The group gradually dispersed from the barn for the remainder of the evening.

3
AMICA TALKS TO JAGO

Draven's report of the drone had rattled Amica. No matter how far she'd come, she couldn't entirely escape the yoke of the city. Its reach was boundless and it had kept a hold of her. It had followed her to the farm, and now it had stake in the others too just to spite her. The group weren't aware of her past, of her being a guard, only Jago knew. What would they think of her if they did know? Would they hate her for it? Her new life on the farm had mollified her and was so prepossessing that she hardly thought of the city any more. But the drone had reminded her and now she could think of little else.

She held her child to her chest. His fingers clutched her, his tiny mind peacefully oblivious to her afflictions; he was perfectly selfish. Cato had given her renewed purpose and a happiness that blighted all else. But she felt she didn't deserve it. She didn't deserve him, or the farm, Jago, or the others either. She thought again of the friends she'd left behind. Why should she be here and they still be there? Why should she cradle a child when they never could? She remembered them, the ones she'd chosen Jago instead of. A year had passed since she'd last seen them. Was the drone an omen, she wondered; her selfishness manifest? Deserting the others was her heaviest cross.

She stared at Cato's small round face, his eyes were shut tightly. With his existence, she was laid bare, no words, no reasoning could defend her against his innocence. Cato could never know, but he was her judge. And looking at him now, she had no choice.

She had to go back for them.

A few days from her resolution, Amica had come up with a plan for returning to the city. She enlisted only Hya to help her, not wanting to task any of the others and upset the balance on the farm. The plan was for them to retrace the journey that the writers had taken back under the city. But this time, they would resurface sooner, at the station closest to Amica's old residence. From her interactions with Talon, Hya was the most knowledgeable of the subway and so would be able to help navigate. From the station, they'd find the others; they all lived in Amica's district and Amica knew where. They would leave tomorrow at dawn, which should see them arrive just after dusk, where the cover of darkness would aid them.

Amica approached Jago to tell him about her plans. The two of them excused themselves from the rest of the group and walked to their outbuilding for privacy. Amica then told Jago she was going back to the city and his response surprised her. He was adamant not only that she should not go, but that not one of them should ever return there. He was reproving of the idea with a frankness that was unlike him. She knew this was causing him great consternation.

'Sacrificing everything we have built here will not help any of them,' he said, 'We are building a future *here*,' - he had emphasised that last word - 'And what of Cato? And the others? You're just going to leave, walk right back to the city and hand yourself to them on a plate? They'll have no mercy, no forgiveness, you'll be done for.'

'I have to,' she cut in, 'They're my friends, they're trapped there.'

Jago looked away, then sat down, collecting himself.

'Your friends?' he said, 'You've hardly mentioned them, and now you're going to risk your life for them?'

'I don't talk about them because I can't *face* talking about them. I left them behind, and I ran away...with you, remember.'

Jago sighed and turned back to her.

'Are you sure they even want your help?' he said, more sympathetically now.

'Yes, they will, I know they will,' she said, sitting down beside him, 'Look at Hya and the others, not one of them wanted to stay behind, they all escaped together.'

Jago started to shake his head.

'I just... I think... The people there are brainwashed, they're too far gone. They're too busy looking at their screens to notice what's happened to them, or to even care. I think they will just tell you to go away.'

She looked at him.

'*You* didn't, Jago, you didn't tell me to go away,' she remonstrated, 'And they won't either. You just have to believe that people still want to help themselves. I know that now.'

Jago took her hand in his and looked back at her.

'You can't save everyone, Amica,' he said, 'You've done enough.'

She stroked his hand with her thumb tenderly and their heads came together in a show of affection.

She thought through all of Jago's council and he was right. She cherished what they had built on the farm and the life they now had. She knew she would be jeopardising all of it; if the worst should happen, she would leave a motherless child and a broken man. She wished she didn't have to choose, she wished she could forget all about her friends, but she couldn't.

They came apart and she looked lovingly back at him.

'I have to try,' she said.

4
HYA SHARES WITH THE WRITERS

The day before Hya and Amica were due to leave for the city, Hya had gathered the writers together away from the barn. They looked at each other and noticed the absence of Jago and Amica and they were intrigued to find out why Hya had asked only them. They sat in a semi circle, some seated on bales, some on blankets on the grass, facing Hya, who was seated in front of them. She was looking down at the ground, and was fidgeting; adjusting constantly and her knee shook from her toe. She hadn't looked up at them once as they'd arrived.

The group settled. Hya started to speak.

'I'm going with Amica to the city just before sunrise,' she told them, as she scuffed some stones with her foot. 'We're taking plenty of supplies. And we're taking Rogue and Calix too. So don't worry about us. We'll be fine.'

'You're going back to the city?' said Otto.

'How?' asked Ever.

'Back through the underground,' replied Hya.

'That's almost a week's hike there and back.'

'Only to get back to our building, we don't need to go back that far,' she corrected Ever, 'It will only be a couple of days.'

'What about light down there, we threw all our phones away,' questioned Annia.

'Amica has torches, with the tools she has.' Hya was fielding their questions.

There was a hesitation as the group tried to think of more to ask her.

'...And...and what will you do when you get there?' came Annia's second query.

'Amica knows some people, a guy called Paine, I think, and some others,' Hya explained, 'We're going to bring them back with us, back here.'

'Bring them *what*?' challenged Otto.

'Isn't that kinda dangerous?' Ever fussed.

'Yes,' Hya confirmed, still fixated on the ground below her, now she was rolling stones back and forth under her foot.

'Okay, sounds a bit suicidal, but sure, if you want to,' Otto summarised bluntly, lifting himself up off the bale to leave. He paused momentarily as Hya spoke again.

'But there is something else I wanted to say to you,' she said. Then her leg stopped moving and she lifted a hand to the back of her head and started to scratch instead. 'I've-I've been thinking about this for a long time and...I-I should tell you all something.'

She sounded tentative and the group were confused, Hya usually spoke so plainly and economically, it was unlike her to be so unsure of herself.

Then she stopped scratching.

'I started the fire in our building,' she declaimed.

The group looked around at each other again, not sure what to make of this.

None of them responded.

Hya carried on, thinking she needed to fill the silence.

'I just wanted-wanted to see what would happen...and maybe see some actual people for once in my life...or at least be outside, maybe...something, I don't know, I-I just couldn't keep sitting there every day, all day, stuck inside, you know, so...so...'

Her utterances trailed off.

There was silence again.

'Was that supposed to be some kind of confession?' Otto said at last, 'Fine by me, I'm glad you did it,' and he resumed walking away.

The rest of the group were not so vocal. The revelation had seemed to numb them.

Hya returned to scratching the back of her head vigorously. Then she looked up at them. She saw all blank faces looking back. Their reaction was one of odd uninvestment, not at all what she'd predicted. She thought they'd be mad at her, or maybe some would comfort her, or perhaps they'd laugh it off, or at the very least, they might ask some more questions.

She'd had enough of this pantomime. She'd talked herself into doing it and now she regretted it.

'So that's it,' she said capriciously, standing up abruptly and turning from them, 'Just wanted to tell you,' and she walked briskly away.

The rest of them sat dumbfounded as they watched her go.

'See you in a few days,' they heard in the distance, as Hya muttered on her way back to the barn.

5
BOOKS

1
RETURN TO THE UNDERGROUND

When the writers regaled Amica and Jago with stories of their emancipation there was one constant: Hya was always spoken highly of. If she was there to hear their pailfuls of praise, she was always uncomfortably bashful. Amica, on the other hand, when Jago lauded *her* achievements, would revel in the adulation, even playing up to her character of *daring rescuer*. Hya envied how this natural amiability of Amica's had ingratiated her with the writers. She had known them for far longer, but Hya felt she'd always struggled in this regard, tending to think they viewed her, even now, as something of a leader figure. Otto was the one exception; they had an affinity; their relationship felt uncomplicated and there was no need for pretence between them. When Hya had admitted to the others her responsibility for the fire in their building, she'd thought this might depose her from the elevated station they'd given her, and bring her closer to them. But when she was met with only silence, she felt nothing would change.

However, unbeknown to Hya, Amica harboured jealousy of *her* also. Namely, she admired Hya for having moved on from her life in the city. She seemed to hold no grudge and was able to focus solely on the here and now, an ability that Amica was lacking. But more importantly, she envied Hya for succeeding where she hadn't: Hya had led the writers to safety from the city, Amica had left *her* group behind.

Despite what they coveted of the other, Hya and Amica would always be married by what they'd achieved in escaping the city. They would always be bound in mutual respect.

Having left first thing, their hike back to the outstation had taken them into the early afternoon. They had left weighed down by their supplies but already, the load had lightened as they had taken refreshments along the way. With them were Rogue and Calix, the dogs. Rogue was the largest and could help protect them, and Calix, with his keen sense of smell, could alert them to possible danger, particularly in the tunnels. Amica and Hya had also brought a ball to throw for them. Rogue had chased it so tirelessly all day that even Hya's gelidity had weathered in the face of his endearing keenness.

The company of the dogs was also a useful distraction for them, what conversation they'd had so far, had been disjointed. The two of them weren't used to being alone together. But, as they neared the station, a topic of genuine interest for Amica came to mind.

'How are you and Rumer then?' she asked Hya.

'Fine, yes,' Hya replied, with a curtness that suggested that they might not be.

There was a long pause as Amica thought of a follow up question, and as she went to ask it, Hya cut her off.

'She's very young, isn't she...'

Amica frowned, 'Aren't you two about the same age?'

'Well, ok, she's young minded then.'

Amica thought about how to respond to this diplomatically, and she said, 'We've all been through a lot, and people react in different ways. I think she'll grow up pretty fast.'

'Yep, she's fine. But...she just seems to expect something from me all the time and I don't know what. As if I'm supposed to say something to her. It's kind of annoying.'

Amica thought again, then suggested, 'Perhaps she has an idealised version of the two of you, and the reality is not quite the same.'

Hya turned to her, 'That's pretty deep,' she said, then turned back, 'I guess I just want to relax now, not have to think about things too much, you know. We made it, we shouldn't be stressed any more.'

'Well I think it'll be good to get some time away. Get some space from each other for a while.'

'Sure.'

There was another pause.

'It's just the group always looked to me for everything,' Hya carried on, 'Like I'm some kind of leader, but, but I just want to be one of them.'

Amica noticed this had become about something more than just Rumer.

'You're over thinking it,' she said pacifically, 'I don't think they see you like that at all, you're more a part of the group than anyone.' She smiled at Hya, trying to placate her.

Hya smiled back, but it was really just to indulge Amica, her opinion hadn't been changed.

'Who is this Paine then, this group you know?' Hya asked Amica as they approached the outstation entrance.

'Paine? He's a delivery driver, we met outside my building when he was on his rounds.'

'A *delivery driver*?'

'Yes,' said Amica, 'You know when you press those buttons on your screen, someone else has to actually do something.'

'Yes, I know,' responded Hya, a little shortly.

'Well, anyway, he'd formed a group, a kind of network with some others. Probably a bit like your one. Whoever dared to speak to him when he was on duty, he would tell them about it - if he felt he could trust them. There were ten of us in the end. We even met up very occasionally, I mean, actually in person.'

'Right, there were ten of us too,' Hya paused, 'And you're sure they'll come back with us?'

'Yes, definitely,' Amica asserted.

'So how do we find them?'

'They're not far from the station. We all live in the same area, that's how Paine got to meet them, on his delivery route. I know where their units are. We'll go and get each of them.'

Amica had elided that she'd scanned each of their phones when she'd met them and found their unit numbers on the safety database.

'Looks like it'll be a long night then,' said Hya, somewhat excited by the prospect.

They pushed passed some striated vines that had grown back over the entrance and they descended down the stairwell to the subway, each step echoing louder than the last. They reached the main tunnel and Amica took out two torches for them from her bag, handing one to Hya.

When they'd walked a little further and the dogs were trotting along happily just ahead, Hya, feeling as if she owed Amica some reciprocal interest in *her* life, asked a question of her own.

'And how is Cato?'

'Yep, good,' Amica responded, 'I mean, he's a baby, so it's hard to tell.'

Hya snorted, finding Amica's flippancy amusing. She much preferred a brusque Amica to a toadying one, like earlier.

Amica smiled then added more seriously, 'Yes, he's fine. There's so much support. He's becoming quite the centre of attention, hope he doesn't get a big head. But no, it's great, it's like he has nine people caring for him.'

'Well, eight,' Hya said perceptively.

Amica smirked.

'Right, I never see you with him,' she said, 'You don't like children much then?'

'Well, they're a bit annoying, and really noisy.'

It was Amica's turn to laugh. She appreciated Hya's honesty.

'Yes,' she said, grinning, 'Yes, I suppose they are.'

2
CHURCH SPIRE

Jago woke. He didn't need to look beside him, he knew she'd already gone. The balance of the bed, the position of the sheets; Amica was no longer beside him. For the rest of the morning, he kept thinking of her and what might happen. She was heading right into the tractor of the city and his pessimism was running rampant. He kept picturing her capture and her correction, he couldn't get it out of his head.

He needed distraction.

He decided he would journey up river the next day. The group often chartered new territory for supplies or materials they could use, and Jago planned to go further than any of them had before. He hoped a tough journey might occupy him until Amica's hopefully safe return.

He'd asked who else had wanted to come, Otto, Annia and, to Jago's surprise, Draven accepted his invitation. He would take Hya's place — she usually going with them on such outings. This was the first time Draven had volunteered for such a trip and Jago was heartened by him showing interest.

Otto and Annia, on the other hand, were regulars, and Jago was used to *their* company. He was very fond of both of them and thought they complemented each other well, though they were still yet to admit to their involvement. Otto was to-the-point, sometimes combative but always loyal, and he was brave. Jago had always admired him for this. It was a kind of bravery that was unquestioning; he never seemed to doubt himself. Jago did however, and always had to will himself to do what he thought was just, it wasn't instinctive like it was for Otto. Bravery was a choice for Jago, for Otto, it just seemed innate.

Then there was Annia; intelligent and perceptive, and a person of unpretentious probity. She and Jago would discuss all manner of things when the group would meet and he always enjoyed their talks. She could be blunt sometimes too, and argumentative, especially when it came to matters of the group. It was in their mutual disputatiousness that her and Otto seemed to found their attraction to one another. They mostly appeared to communicate through a sort of badinage; where one would antagonise the other, then the other would riposte. Both were highly engaging and this magnetism drew and kept them together.

With Annia and Otto certain to spend the journey in the pocket of the other, Jago knew he would be walking alongside Draven. Draven had largely removed himself from the group since the loss of his close friends, Caius and Ophelia, and was usually chained to his work. He had been invaluable in creating all manner of things for the group, particularly equipment for the farm, which had been revolutionary. They were all in his debt and they wished there was some way to show their gratitude. It had not come as a complete shock to Jago that Draven had wanted to come. The group were starting to see a little more of him at meal times and also with Cato, whom he'd become very fond of, even making him a few basic toys to play with.

The following day, they set off, and as expected, Annia and Otto had taken the lead together, with Jago and Draven walking just behind them.

'Draven, we haven't spoken for a while,' Jago said a short way into the trip, 'How are you?'

'Yes, I'm fine, how about yourself?'

'Not bad,' Jago replied litotically. He realised he always spoke to Draven in a slightly feigned manner. He hoped it never came across as patronising. 'What have you been doing?' he added, trying to sound more casual.

'Oh, not too much,' said Draven, 'Working on some new projects, the usual.'

'Right,' Jago responded, 'Where did you learn all that stuff by the way? Most of us wouldn't know where to start.'

'Well, I was an engineer in the old world,' he said matter-of-factly, 'They had me working on all sorts; machines mainly, vehicles, that kind of thing, boring stuff really. You know the old trains? Well, some of that was me.' He turned to Jago and raised his eyebrows. 'All back in the day, of course.'

'Of course,' Jago repeated.

'I've been doing some writing too,' he continued, Jago noticing he didn't need any prompting this time, 'With some of the stuff Hya brought with her.'

'Really...,' Jago sounded intrigued.

'Yes, just some stories and the like.'

'No end to your talents.'

'I'm sure there is, but it passes the time.'

'Mm, so what are you writing about?'

'Well actually, I've been writing up some of Ophelia's and Caius's old stories, the ones they used to regale us with, all about the old world, what they used to get up to, etcetera. You remember?'

Jago was about to correct him before Draven realised his miscalculation.

'Oh no, sorry,' he said, 'you wouldn't have really heard them, would you.'

'No, I'm afraid not. I didn't get to know them very well unfortunately. But,' he looked at Draven, 'but now I can, right, with your writing. I can read all about them.'

'Yes, that's true,' Draven agreed with an uplifted timbre, he seemed pleased to hear this.

As the two of them walked, they could hear the chatter and occasional guffaw of laughter from up ahead. Otto and Annia were overtly fraternising in front of them.

Then they hushed suddenly and stopped moving.

'You see what I'm seeing?' Otto shouted out loud to every one.

In the distance, there was a spire crescendoing out from amongst a line of tree tops.

'You don't see that everyday,' he added.

'A church spire,' said Annia, 'There's got to be a village there.'

Respecting it was still *his* expedition, the two of them turned to Jago and he saw the look of hopeful enquiry on their faces.

He glanced at Draven, who shrugged. 'All right, let's take a look,' Jago said, acquiescing to the two in front.

They continued on towards the trees, the river they were following still running parallel to them. The spire they'd seen loomed over them as they entered the woods. It continually beckoned them, but never seemed to get any closer. Finally, they came out from the cover of the trees and a row of stone buildings were waiting for them. They lined either side of a central pathway, leading to a raised courtyard.

'There's at least twenty houses here,' Jago pronounced, taking it all in, 'And more over there,' he pointed down another path leading off from the main street.

The four of them were in awe of the quaint visage of the rural idyll they had stumbled upon. They went a little further towards the courtyard and the rest of the church was revealed to them from behind the row of houses.

'Never seen anything like it,' Otto commented, so transfixed by it, he tripped slightly on the stones.

They continued down the path, passing each building one by one, all of them unique. Years of disregard had engulfed them in overgrown wisteria and untempered climbers. The vegetation was so abundant, the cottage-like structures looked as if they could have sprouted up from the earth itself.

'Were you born somewhere like this then, Jago?' asked Annia.

'Not as nice as this, no,' he replied, 'But in the countryside, yes.'

They came into the courtyard, a kind of village square at the foot of the church. They looked up at it.

'Magnificent,' Draven remarked.

The four of them stood, torpid for a while, unable to look away.

'We should get back before nightfall,' Otto said eventually, the first to remember their purpose — at least the three of *theirs* — 'Not sure if I fancy desecrating a church, but there must be loads of stuff elsewhere we can use. So where do we start? How about there?' and he pointed to the building nearest.

Jago panned down from the church to him, then across to the rectory where he was pointing.

'Yes, let's take a look,' he concurred, 'Draven, see if there's anything you want from there too.'

Draven nodded.

Jago took a few steps towards the rectory. 'But,' he paused, 'I'm going to take a look inside the church after, if anyone wants to join...'

'I will,' said Annia.

Jago continued on with Annia and Otto joining. But this time Draven spoke, stopping them again. The three of them turned to him.

'Something monumental about it, isn't there,' he said, 'Something anachronistic: it's been there for hundreds of years, hosted tens of thousands of people and witnessed so much history. And it's still standing, immutable and enduring.'

3
THE NEW FAMILY

Amica's plan to return to the city was never realised. Her and Hya had travelled only a short way underground when Calix became restless. He began to scrap for their attention, running around their legs and jumping up on them. Then he sprinted off into the darkness where the torches could not reach him. Hya immediately signalled the larger dog to go after him, and Rogue set off too. Amica and Hya then followed the noise of their barking. They turned from the main tunnel and into a narrow conduit, where their lights revealed the dogs again. They were barking vociferously at a hatchway they'd discovered. There was some fencing around it that looked temporary, like it had been moved there.

A voice was pleading from inside it.

'Wait, wait!' it said, 'I'm here! I'll come out, I surrender!'

Amica could hear the desperation in the voice. She felt guilty: the dogs must be terrifying.

'Arrow, Calix, quiet!' she hushed. The dogs pipped down but stayed alert. Then she shouted at the hatch, 'We're not here to hurt you. We're not them!'

There was a mechanical clicking sound. The hatch began to open. Amica stood in front of the dogs, shooing them behind her and trying to calm them, 'No, no, friend, friend,' she bargained with them.

A figure edged cautiously out from the enclosure. A frightened face appeared in the torchlight, then hands, which were raised in surrender. Amica realised and lowered her light quickly not to blind him, gesturing for Hya to do the same. The figure closed the door behind him.

'I'll come quietly, let's go, please,' he supplicated, moving towards them.

The dogs growled. Amica waved them down.

'No, no, it's okay, we're here to help,' she explained to him, as diffusively as she could, 'Who are you?'

He looked back at her, frozen for a moment.

'You're not one of them, are you?' he said, 'You're not from the city!'

'No, we're not.'

'Then I'm...,' he sounded tentative, 'I'm Maxen, you-you can call me Max.'

'Hi Max, I'm Amica. This is Hya. And this is Rogue and Calix,' she looked at the dogs, then in an attempt to lighten the situation, she joked, 'They've already said hello.' But there was no reaction.

She inched closer, trying not to startle him.

Max's head twitched from her to the dogs and back again. Then he said suddenly, 'You have to help her!' his tone urgent, 'Can you help her?'

'Who?' Amica asked, concerned.

Max glanced behind him.

'My daughter.'

He turned, reopened the hatch and hurried back through. Hya and Amica went in after him.

There was a small compartment, three others were inside; a young boy standing beside the others, and a woman crouched down over a young girl. The girl was hunched over and wheezing stertorously.

'She needs help, she's struggling to breath,' exclaimed Max.

Amica knelt down by her and checked the girl's breathing. She saw her panicked eyes flick to her, then away again.

'You know what it is?' said the woman crouching.

'I'm not sure...,' Amica said, 'Maybe she's asthmatic... It's the air down here, plus the cold. She can't stay here.'

Amica cradled the girl and lifted her up. Max rushed to object.

'Look there's no time,' Amica tried to explain, 'We have to go, we know the way back up to the surface, where there's no guards. She needs to be outside, she's only going to get worse down here.'

Amica left the compartment with the girl in her arms and hurried back through the conduit. The others followed, huddled around her.

'What's her name?' Amica asked them.

'Freya,' Max replied.

'Hi Freya,' she said, 'We'll take care of you. Just try to relax, and breath slowly.' Amica breathed exaggeratedly to demonstrate.

The three of them continued down the tunnel, Rogue following closely behind.

Hya had come out from the compartment just behind them. Calix was by her side. She watched Amica and the others disappear around the corner to the main tunnel.

She stopped, feeling something wasn't quite right. She swung her torch back around and saw him. The boy was still standing there.

Hya waved him towards her, 'We're going!' she instructed.

He shook his head profusely.

Hya glanced back down the tunnel again, the last of Amica's torchlight was disappearing.

'Come on, we have to go,' she urged.

The boy shook his head again.

Hya was unsure what to do.

Perhaps she might be able to negotiate. She went to him and knelt down in front of him.

'Hi,' she said.

He was looking passed her shoulder to where the others had gone.

'It's okay,' Hya said, 'they didn't forget about you. They're just worried for the girl. Is she your sister?'

He nodded.

'Ok-ok, don't worry. Erm...' Hya couldn't think.

Then Calix wandered over to the two of them and went right up to the boy to investigate him. He twisted slightly away from the interest, but as Calix's fur brushed against his arm, it tickled him and he let out a laugh. Hya could see the dog was befriending him far more quickly than she could. She realised the dog was her best tool for gaining his trust.

'See, he likes you,' she said, 'Say hello to Calix.'

The boy lifted an arm out and petted him gingerly.

Hya smiled, 'See, friendly.'

As he stroked the top of Calix's head, he whispered, 'Hello.'

'Ok, good, good,' said Hya, seeing him speak finally. Her tactic seemed to be working. 'Now Calix wants to know your name too?'

'Fox,' the boy responded, to the dog.

'Okay then Fox, shall we check on your sister? I think she'd like to see you,' said Hya, 'Would you like to go see her? It's okay, Calix will come with us.'

Fox nodded again.

'Ok, good. Do you like running?'

'Yes,' he answered, more confidently this time.

Hya rose to her feet, 'Okay, good, let's catch them up. Calix will lead the way for us. Let's follow him, okay?'

Fox then took Hya's hand. She was taken by surprise but gripped it back. They started to jog down the conduit, Calix running out in front of them as Hya had promised.

'So, it's asthma or something?' Max said, as the three of them paced along the tunnel.

'Or something, yes, I don't know, sorry, I just know she can't stay down here for much longer,' Amica responded, 'Why are you down here anyway?'

'We came down here about a year ago,' Max replied.

'A *year*?' Amica said, surprised, 'How could you survive down here a *year*?'

'There are supplies in the stations...and we go up to the surface when we absolutely have to,' the woman with them explained, both her and Max out of breath now.

'Very resourceful,' Amica remarked. 'What about her?' she added, 'This hasn't happened *before*?'

'Sometimes, but never this bad...,' she answered.

'This is my wife by the way,' Max clarified.

'Jonet,' she introduced herself.

'*Wife*?' said Amica, '...Oh, okay, hi there.'

'And then this is my son—' Max started.

He stopped.

They halted.

'Fox!' yelled Max, his words reverberating down the tunnel, 'Where's Fox?'

Amica looked behind, realising that Hya and Calix were absent too.

'It's fine, Hya will be with him,' she said presuming, 'She's not here either, she wouldn't leave him behind, trust me.'

Then, arriving just on cue, a light emerged in the distance, followed by the figures of Hya, Fox and Calix.

'Fox!' shouted Max and he and Jonet rushed over to embrace him.

'Don't do that,' said Jonet, 'Shout if you're behind.'

They stood back up from him, each holding one of his hands. Then they looked over at Hya.

'Thanks!' Jonet said to her, 'Thanks for watching him.'

Hya nodded. 'No problem,' she said.

4
BODHI

'Can I help?' said a voice from behind them. Jago dropped the drawer he had pulled out from the cabinet. It crashed to the floor. 'You can take what you wish,' it said, 'I don't mind, please be my guest.'

The four of them turned. A tenebrous figure stood in the entrance of the rectory, shrouded by the shadow from its awning. It took a step towards them, and just when they thought the light might reveal him, the shadow moved too. It was as if the light dimmed just for him.

Otto had picked up a measure of wood from the floor, hidden behind his back. 'What do you want?' he said gruffly.

'I don't want anything,' said the voice.

The four of them braced as the figure took another step towards them.

Jago, taking a different tack, tried, 'We escaped from the city. How about you?'

Still there was no response.

Otto was getting frustrated, 'Tell us how you got here?' he demanded. He found he was gripping the plank of wood so tightly, it had cut into his skin.

'I walked,' the voice answered him.

Otto and Jago glanced at each other.

'We...we came here by accident,' Jago continued calmly, determined to keep the peace, 'We're just looking for supplies. We are not here to do anyone any harm.'

'I know,' the voice said.

Jago couldn't see the eyes of their interloper, but somehow, he still felt he was being studied.

'Okay, good, I'm Jago,' he introduced the others, 'This is Annia, Otto and Draven.'

The figure took one final step towards them, the light revealing him at last.

'I'm Bodhi,' he said.

Since they'd first turned to him, Jago had been thinking of Amica's designs on expanding the group. If they were ever to come across anyone else, she had always wanted to take them in and help them if they could. Perhaps Bodhi was one such person.

'Hi Bodhi,' he said, 'We, we have a group, and a home. It's not much, but we have food, water and shelter. You can...you can join us if you want...'

There was a pause. Bodhi looked at him. He was completely expressionless.

'I too have food, water and shelter,' he replied, 'and no one else to divide them between. I have plenty, too much if anything. But I thank you for your kind offer.'

'You seem very calm for someone who's just run into four complete strangers...,' said Annia, interjecting.

Bodhi turned to her, 'No point in being overly stressed, is there.'

She agreed with the sentiment, but was no less suspicious of his serenity.

'Guess not,' she mumbled, feeling she needed to say something.

'Anyway,' said Bodhi, sounding as if he was concluding, 'Like I say, take what you like for your group and your home, I have plenty to go around. You are more than welcome and I wish you the best of luck.'

He turned away and left. He was unhurried and passed slowly through the shadow and back out into the light of the outside.

'Interesting guy,' Otto joked, once he was out of ear shot.

The four of them couldn't help but now feel they were trespassing on someone else's delimitation. The village was no longer unspoken for and they decided they should leave.

They tidied up the leftover mess they'd created, rounding up what they already had into their bags and hoisting them onto their shoulders. They went back out to the village square where Jago and Annia eyed up the church again, deciding they could not resist a look inside.

'We'll be quick,' said Jago, 'We'll go home straight after.'
They put their bags back down and headed towards it.
'Jago?' Draven said.
'Yes?' said Jago, turning back.
'It-it just feels odd leaving him here, all alone.'
Jago sighed, having had the same thought. 'I know, but he doesn't want to join us, Draven. But…how about…how about we come back and check on him some day, how about that?'
Draven agreed, 'Yes, okay.'
'Jago,' Otto jumped in, 'this village would make a really nice place to live.'
Jago looked at him, 'Yes, I know, but it's not ours.'
They heard footsteps and down the path approached Bodhi again. He came up to them. They waited for him to speak, but he said nothing.
'Was there something else?' Jago asked him.
'Draven,' said Bodhi, ignoring Jago, 'May I show you something?'
Draven was surprised to be singled out. He looked at Jago, unsure what to make of the invite. Jago shrugged, unable to offer any guidance.
Draven turned back to Bodhi. 'Okay,' he said.
Bodhi then walked passed them and up the slope to the church, seeming not to acknowledge the other three. He continued into the churchyard, then turned and beckoned for Draven to follow him, which he did.
The others watched as they went inside.
'I'm not sure about this,' Annia said.
'You're not sure about anything,' Otto said impudently.
'I mean, we don't know who he is,' she added, trying her best to ignore him.
'C'mon, what's he gonna do,' Otto argued, 'Look, he'll shout if he needs us.'
'Hope so,' Annia said under her breath.
They sat down on the benches around the square in wait.
'I think you might have to forget about our tour of the church though, Annia,' said Jago.

Meanwhile, Bodhi and Draven had reached the chancel when Bodhi stopped, Draven nearly bumping into him as he followed behind.

Bodhi turned to face him.

'You were the only one who didn't speak before, in the rectory,' he said, 'Are you okay?'

'Me?' Draven said without thinking.

'Yes, I see you all standing there, and I see the other one hold that piece of wood behind him, and I feel unease, perhaps even fear from the other three. But you, I feel nothing from you. You don't flinch, you don't react. It's like you didn't care what was happening, like you weren't present in the situation. You were elsewhere somehow.'

Draven, not sure how to respond, said the first thing that came to mind.

'I've just been trying to get my head around everything,' - he knew he was obfuscating - 'We've had such a strange journey, all of us.'

'I don't doubt that.'

Bodhi turned and continued down the aisle and through to the vestruary. Draven followed him to a doorway, where Bodhi stopped again.

'I wanted to show you something,' he said. He pushed the door open. It creaked noisily. 'In here.'

Draven looked through into what he presumed was a lady chapel of sorts. It was too dark to see but a pungent smell of old wood and dank filled his nostrils. It was reminiscent of something, though he wasn't exactly sure what. The two of them went inside, the door creaking closed behind them.

They were in pitch black. Then, a light flashed, imprinting on Draven's retina for a moment. Bodhi had struck a match. Then he lit a candle and the room came to life. Draven saw the walls, they were all lined with shelves, and on them, sat rows and rows of books.

'I-I can't believe it,' he stuttered in astonishment, trying to suppress conniptions of excitement.

He looked back at Bodhi. His face was still expressionless, but Draven swore he saw some sojourning satisfaction run across it.

Bodhi motioned with his hand, as if to say, *take a look*. Draven didn't know where to begin. He went to the nearest shelf, reached out and ran his finger along one of the rows of books. He paused on one at random, then moved his finger down its spine.

'I didn't think I'd ever see one of these again,' he said.

He drew the book he had fingered from the shelf. He felt the weight of the tome as he held it, it even surprising him a little. He opened it and the weight distributed satisfyingly out to its two planes. He felt the page, it was worn and rough to the touch. He followed a line of writing with his finger and it removed the dust; a line of brightness was left across the paper and a yellow dust secreted on his finger. He then closed the book and heard and felt the thud of the pages coming together. He placed it back on the shelf, pushing it exactly level with the others, as it slid pleasingly into its place.

'How old are they?' Draven queried.

'I don't know.'

'Have you read all of them?'

'Most of them, yes. Nothing but time on my hands these days, of course.'

Draven scanned over the books once again, estimating how many there might be. 'It's as if they're documents of the past, isn't it,' he thought out loud, 'You can't alter them, can't edit them, they're sempiternal.'

He pulled another book from a different shelf. With this one, he noticed a purple ribbon looped out of the spine. He picked at it, fed it out from the front page. He opened the book and placed the ribbon about half way into it, pulling it down into the fold. He was fascinated by its simple efficiency. He closed the book back up over the ribbon.

'You didn't have them in the city, did you?' Bodhi asked.

'No, not allowed,' responded Draven, 'Well, not real ones.'

Draven then reconsidered Bodhi's question, the books had distracted him.

'What do you mean *you didn't have them…*?' he said, turning to him, 'How couldn't you have known that?'

Bodhi looked at him for a moment.

'Oh, I was never in the city,' he said, realising what Draven was getting at.

A puzzled frown appeared on Draven's face. 'How were you never in the city?' he asked.

'I have been out here my whole life. I was never taken to the city. When they came, I was able to hide in the woods and they couldn't find me. I was the only one who was suspicious, you see, the others all made themselves known.'

Whilst Draven considered this, Bodhi then revisited one of *Draven's* comments, something occurring to *him*.

'Draven?' he said with interest, 'What do you mean by *real ones*?'

'*Real ones…*?' he glanced at him, '…Oh, I see, we only had digital books in the city.'

'Well at least that's something,' said Bodhi.

'Not really, we were only allowed ones that had been approved. They're pretty much all from the last few years. Most books were banned you see, the older ones especially…like these ones.'

Draven looked for a reaction to this. Bodhi's countenance was unmoved as usual, but he knew this had upset him.

Bodhi looked down as if he were thinking deeply, 'That's terrible,' he sighed.

'Yes, it is,' Draven said, placing the book in his hand back on the shelf.

Bodhi then seemed to reset from his momentary cogitation.

'Would you like to take one with you?' he offered.

'Really? Are you sure?'

'Of course, be my guest.'

'They're all so old,' Draven pointed out, looking over them, 'I don't know where to begin.'

'Not all of them, this one's newer.' Bodhi reached across Draven and drew out from a lower shelf a much thinner book, looking far younger than the rest. 'Why don't you start here, it's a little more demotic, I believe one of the villagers wrote it.' He passed the book to Draven. 'It's about the city.'

Draven took the book and nodded in appreciation.

He appraised the cover and the back.

'It looks as if it could be brand new,' he said, then opened it and flicked through some pages. 'Wait, how...? ...This is handwritten...in ink!' he gasped. He looked at Bodhi for confirmation.

Bodhi nodded.

Draven placed the donation carefully into his jacket pocket, finding it fit there neatly.

'Thank you,' he said with earnest.

The others turned as the hefty doors of the church reopened and Draven and Bodhi came outside into the courtyard. This time it was Draven who stopped. He turned to Bodhi.

'Thank you again for the book,' he said, 'It's great, I look forward to reading it. But...I have to ask, why did you decide to show me the books?'

Bodhi started to respond, 'Because I thought you looked—'

'Yes,' interrupted Draven, 'Because I looked like *I wasn't present*. I know, you wanted to see if I was okay, thank you. But, I mean, why *the books*, why did you think the books specifically would help?'

For the first time, Bodhi looked slightly piqued. He took his time to think.

Jago, Otto and Annia continued to look over at them, it seemed an age before Bodhi replied. Finally he straightened, seemingly happy with what he was going to say.

'When the rest of the village was taken and moved into the city,' he began, 'I missed them. I missed them so much I didn't want to do *anything* any more, nothing at all. So all I could think about was just counting down the time I had left until the day I would die.'

Draven looked back at him humanely. Bodhi continued.

'I kept thinking of my time left to pass as sand in an hourglass; a little cliché, I know. But anyway, I was still so young, and there was so much sand at the top and hardly any at the bottom. And I thought, I can't possibly wait for all that sand to pass through to the bottom. So somehow, I needed to try to forget about the sand in the hourglass, otherwise, I would just go mad thinking about it, no?'

He took a calming breath.

'So, I tried to imagine the hourglass as completely empty, with no sand at all. You see, if there's no sand falling through, then there's no time, yes? If there's no time, there would be no past for me to miss, no present for me to waste and no future for me to worry about. If there is no past, no present and no future, then all memory and thought are meaningless, and all action is inconsequential. If everything has no significance then nothing can weigh you down any more. Right? If nothing has any meaning, then you can't feel anything...'

It was Draven's turn to look blank.

'Anyway,' Bodhi carried on, 'it didn't really work unfortunately, not straight away anyway. I just kept seeing the sand and I kept picturing the motion of it through the hourglass, falling and falling and falling, playing in my head, over and over; forever imposed there and forever animating. It was torment. But then...,' - his voice lifted - 'but then, I found the books in the church. I never knew they were even there, well why would I, I had never gone back there before. And so I read, I just kept reading, I never did anything else but read. Then, you see, I barely noticed the days and the nights passing, I barely noticed anything around me changing. It was like time only passed in the books and had stopped in real life. So, I was able to stop thinking of the past, the past I missed so much, and I ceased counting down the time I had left till death. And, after that, I just felt light and free.

'So, I guess I thought I saw some sadness in you too, when you were in the rectory. You looked...down maybe, like you had lost people too perhaps, just like I had. But, what I'm trying to say is: read that book, read all the books, and it might help you feel better.'

Bodhi then moved closer to Draven and placed a hand on his arm.

'You see, whoever you have lost, Draven, you haven't,' he said, 'They are not gone, because the hourglass is empty. They are still with you now, because there is no sand.'

Draven contemplated all that Bodhi had said. He was moved.

He mirrored Bodhi by putting *his* hand on Bodhi's other arm.

'Thank you, I think I understand,' he said, with a sincere look. And he was certain this time, a glimmer of emotion *did* visit Bodhi's usually inscrutable face.

'You know, that's a lot of information to read into a complete stranger,' Draven joked.

'I know,' Bodhi responded, 'but I was right, right?'

'Mm, maybe.'

Draven smiled then brought a close to their interview, nodding at Bodhi and walking passed him back towards the others. They stood up, picking their bags up in readiness.

Draven paused after a few paces and turned back to Bodhi a final time.

'By the way,' he said, 'we thought we'd come back some day and see you. Do you mind?'

'Of course, be my guest.'

5
LOOKING AFTER FREYA AND FOX

'Boil water,' Amica shouted to anyone who was close enough to hear.

Ever reacted fastest, handing Cato over to Cleo, *I'll go*, he said and rushed off to the barn. Cleo stood up, now with the baby in her arms and watched as Amica came at a canter towards them. She was carrying a small child and there were two others with her. They weren't part of the group.

Amica placed the girl on the grass just as Ever returned with a bowl of steaming water. She was positioned with her head over the bowl and a towel over her head. Amica told her to take deep breaths as she massaged her back to help her circulation.

'What's going on?' said Ever to Amica, seeing the girl and the new people.

'I think she's fine,' Amica responded, 'They were underground and...she was having trouble breathing but...,' - Amica was catching her breath - 'she felt better as soon as we came up...to the surface.'

Ever nodded, glancing at the other two, but they were occupied.

Amica, seeing Cleo holding Cato just away from them, gestured to the man next to her to continue massaging, demonstrating the motion for him. She got to her feet and went over to them.

'Is he okay?' she said to Cleo.

'Yes, he's fine,' Cleo responded, handing the baby over to his mother.

'Where's Jago?' Amica said, placing Cato on her hip.

'He wanted to go search a new area or something, Annia, Otto, Draven went with him.'

'*Draven* went?'

But Cleo was too distracted. The returning dogs had come bounding over to her. She knelt down and petted them with rapture. Arrow then joined them from behind the barn and the pack was reunited.

'Is everyone else okay?' Amica continued, seeing Ever come back over.

'Yes, we're all good, don't worry,' he said, 'We weren't expecting you back for ages?'

'Yes, well, we had some unforeseen circumstances,' Amica freed a hand and motioned at the strangers, 'We bumped into them, quite early on on the way. Like I say, the girl, she was ill, we had to come straight back.'

'Right,' said Ever, trying to picture what had happened.

Amica then lifted Cato up and embraced him, holding him tightly to her and squeezing him. The relief from seeing him flooded through her. She held him out in front of her, grinned at him. She was thankful to be home again.

'It's okay, keep breathing,' Max said, as he continued to rub Freya's back the way Amica had shown him. He looked over at Amica, who was standing just away from them. He then further delegated massaging duties to Jonet, showing her the same technique he had. He stood up and went over to Amica and the others.

'Hi, I'm Maxen, Max,' he said to the two he didn't know, they smiled back, then turning to Amica, he added humbly, 'Thank you again.'

'You're welcome,' Amica said back, still engaged with Cato.

Max was struck by what he was seeing; the once purposeful and staid stranger that had rescued his daughter from the underground, was now glowing exuberantly and playing cutely with a baby.

'Hi Max,' then came a welcoming voice, 'I'm Ever, this is Cleo and the little one's Cato. Just ask if any of you want food or water, I will get you whatever you need.'

'Oh, thank you,' Max responded gratefully, nodding at him and Cleo.

Amica looked at Ever after this display of hospitality and civility and felt a parental pride. How he had had to mature in such ill affording time, she thought; the harshest of trial had placed a worldly head on young shoulders.

Rumer was woken from her nap by the commotion. She heard new voices and went outside. On seeing the girl, she immediately went to tend to her and during her short convalescence, Rumer brought fresh water and offered her many words of encouragement. By the late morning, Freya was talking with almost no trace of her ailments. Rumer was warmed by her rambunctious twaddle as she cawed often, despite a still hoarse voice, at anyone and everyone who would listen; there was no lack of confidence in her now. The two of them bonded quickly over this abounding unfettered chatter. Rumer was delighted to have found a cohort in the new young arrival.

It wasn't until later when she was still with Freya, that Rumer realised she was yet to see Hya since the others had returned.

She stood up in the field and on tip toe swivelled around to scan the area for her.

There she was, sat in the distance on a row of bales. She was not alone. There beside her, was seated a small figure. His feet did not reach the ground, neither did his knees reach the corner of the bale, so his legs stuck out comically from his body.

Rumer filled with excitement and rushed over to them.

'Hi!' she said as she approached.

Both barely reacted. A quiet, *hi*, was all Hya could muster.

The boy, seeing Hya's standoffishness and seeming to intuit the friction between the two adults, shifted closer to Hya on the bale. He then looked up, shooting Rumer a childish glare.

Undeterred by him, Rumer said to Hya, 'I'm glad you're okay.'

'I am,' Hya huffed.

After a moment, Rumer turned back to the boy, wondering if she might have more luck with *him*.

'And what's your name?' she said — her voice entering that higher register reserved for children, still involuntarily after so many years without them.

The boy was still guarded, a frown seeming permanently pasted on his forehead. He looked up at Hya for direction.

'It's okay,' Hya advised, 'We know her. She lives here too.'

He turned back to Rumer.

'Fox,' he said cagily

'Hi Fox, I'm Rumer,' she said to him, as enthusiastically as she could.

But that was the most she got out of him. He resumed his obstinateness and didn't say another word to her.

Rumer looked at Hya.

'Well, at least he seems to like *you*,' she said.

Hya looked away. 'I don't know,' she responded curtly.

Fox then crossed his arms impiously and glared up at Rumer once more; he had firmly chosen Hya's side in whatever fracture there was between the two grown ups.

Rumer was bemused by him and couldn't help but laugh; Hya, of all people, who was somewhat contemptuous of children, had seemed to have garnered the affections, and the chivalry, of this one.

'Mm, interesting,' she said, to no one in particular.

Later that day, the search group of Jago, Annia, Otto and Draven also returned to the farm. Everyone gathered around the barn, feeling a debriefing ought to be had. After general introductions were made between the returning group and the new family, everyone moved inside. The floor was given to Jonet and Max and they began to explain how they came to be found in the tunnel by Amica and Hya.

Shortly into their retelling, Freya and Fox had fallen asleep in the corner of the barn. They were exhausted. Their parents let them be, thinking that with their impressionable ears absent, the general discussion might be more lubricated.

'Fox had just turned ten and,' Jonet was saying, 'and he was selected for the project. It was coming to the day when they would take him away…and…,' her voice started to crack.

'We couldn't let them take him, there was no way,' said Max.

'We'd heard all the spiel,' Jonet continued a moment later, *'It's a better life for them, they're saving the city...* but we'd stopped believing all that a long time ago.

'We knew about the education camps, the training, what they put them through. They turn them into tools of the city. We heard they're never the same again.

'We couldn't have Fox be one of them. And Freya? In two years, she could be selected too, then she'd be taken. We'd never see either of them again.'

'They say they come back when they're older,' Max added, 'But they never do, they're too far gone. There's no *coming back* from it.'

'What happens to them?' Otto asked the couple.

'No one's really sure exactly,' Jonet answered, 'All I know is they get trained and go work for the city. Some become guards, some run the trains, the cars, some of them join the nudge team. But they don't tell you, of course, we'd never know what Fox was doing, or where he was.'

Otto looked over at Amica. 'Amica, you seem to know the most about the city, you know much about it?'

The rest of the group turned to Amica. She was staring vacantly to the back of the barn.

She sensed the attention on her.

'What?' she said.

'The kids,' Otto reiterated, 'When they're ten, what happens if they're selected and leave their homes, you know much about it...?'

Amica shrugged. 'Don't know,' she muttered dismissively.

The others looked at her: it was an uncharacteristic response. The barn fell quiet.

Then Jago jumped in.

'So then you escaped to the underground when you found out?' he said to Max and Jonet.

'Er...yes,' Max replied, moving on as Jago had hoped, 'It was that or lose Fox forever. We didn't know where we were going but we made it down there. We found some supplies at the first station we came across, even some emergency lighting we could use. And then, we just stayed there, in that compartment, put that fence around it. We didn't think anyone would bother coming after us. We didn't have a plan, just stay down there as long as we could so they couldn't get Fox...or Freya.' He paused, remembering the encounter in the tunnel, 'And then, we saw the lights...and heard those dogs, and we thought-we-we thought that was it, we were done for...'

Jonet put her arm around Max.

Amica was too detached to sympathise with the piteous couple, despite feeling she should.

'We can't thank you enough, Amica,' Jonet said, looking over at her, 'I think you may have saved Freya's life.'

Amica turned away, feeling all the eyes of the room on her again.

'Thank Calix,' she said ungraciously, 'He found you.'

A few of the group laughed hesitantly. Jonet wasn't sure how to take the comment.

Jago saw the defensiveness from Amica and knew talk of the city was nettling her.

'And thanks to Hya too,' Max carried on, turning to *her* now, 'We thought Fox was right behind us. Thank you so much for staying with him.'

Hya cordially nodded back at them.

The group collectively breaked, some getting water and some, food. They reconvened inside the barn, finding roughly their same positions. The discussion continued, with Max and Jonet the focus as before.

'So,' Max deflected after a few more questions, 'What are all *your* stories? How did you all get out?'

The group waited for someone to answer. Jago went first.

'Amica and I got out over a year ago. We met in the city and escaped together,' - he was being careful not to divulge too much information - 'As for every one else,' he gestured around at the others, 'Well, we actually met them in *this* barn for the first time...'

He looked at the group, wanting one of them to take over from him. None of them did.

Max spoke instead.

'So, so the rest of you are all together? How did you all meet?'

Otto then pipped up, rather unceremoniously.

'Hya tried to set us all on fire!' he announced.

His bombastic delivery had the group rolling around in cachinnations.

Max and Jonet looked on, not sure why this was so funny; they must have missed something.

'Set you on fire?' said Jonet, shocked.

'It's a long story,' Otto replied, smirking knowingly.

Hya wasn't joining in with the laughter. 'That's not what happened,' she said under her breath.

The group simmered down a little noticing Hya wasn't partaking in the joviality.

Discussion continued into the early evening until Jago, reminded by the failing light, called a close to the meeting. The group started to disperse around the barn, some going outside.

Jago turned to Max and Jonet.

'Well, everyone has interesting stories like that, so, you know, just ask them,' he said, 'Anyway, we'll set you up somewhere to sleep in here. Looks like the kids have already reserved their spaces.'

The couple smiled at him as the three of them observed Fox and Freya still fast asleep in the corner.

Draven, who had stayed behind, touched Jago on the arm to get his attention.

'They can have the outhouse,' Draven said to Jago as he turned to him.

Jonet and Max overheard and looked enquiringly at Draven.

'Um, you can have the building out there,' Draven repeated to them, 'I'll move into the barn. It doesn't make sense me using it on my own. You should have it.'

Jago nodded in approval of the idea.

'Are you sure?' Max asked Draven.

'Yes,' he confirmed.

'Okay, sure, we'll set that up for you,' said Jago, 'Anyway, welcome to the farm.'

6
CLEO HAS A CHILD

Presuming her nausea and lateness only side effects from the revolution in her life, perhaps the most obvious diagnosis hadn't even occurred to Cleo. In solitude most of her life, she'd never thought about children; the certitude of her never meeting anyone physically had been deeply incepted. So it was the rest of the group, once they'd noticed her occasional sickness and incommensurate belly, that felt bound by a duty to inform her she may well be with child. Equally as disbelieving was Ever, her partner, who could never have imagined it either. During their inchoate adulthood, he, and Cleo, had only ever interacted with others online and only there had they observed any past relationships. When the two of them realised, the thought of a child was very disquieting for them. They had lived for so long under city dictate, which rendered all in-person interaction impossible, that the two of them felt they must have wronged in some way. The others had to remind them the city no longer had jurisdiction over them and they were free to carry on whatever relationship they liked. So after much encouragement, Cleo and Ever finally came to terms with what was about to happen: they would indeed, have a child.

So to a huge fanfare, Jett was born several months later at the end of autumn. The group were ecstatic for them.

With this new arrival, the group were beginning to consider, for the first time, about the more lasting implications of what they'd started at the farm. There were now four children in the group: the two eldest, rescued in the subway, Fox and Freya, and the two native born, Cato and Jett. In a relatively short span of time, the adults could now see the early semblance of a new generation, one that could potentially follow in their considerable footsteps. With this in mind, they started to think less of their own immediate demands and more of what future they might create.

Draven thought about how Bodhi's ethos of the empty hourglass applied to their now expanding group. He postulated that the arrival of the children was metaphorically the removing of the sand from the hourglass; that the group were no longer focused on the finiteness of themselves: the sand passing through, but of the infiniteness of what they might leave behind: the hourglass itself. They now had a sense of timelessness; they were procuring a future, not simply surviving.

Just like with Cato, the entire group adopted Jett as their own. They adored him. Even Hya, who had developed a kind of brooding companionship with Fox, showed some fleeting interest in him. Rumer could swear something of a softer side was emerging in her, though it was not however, Rumer herself that was its benefactor. Hya was still withdrawn from *their* relationship and Rumer didn't know why, which frustrated her. Hya was implacable; she was not interested in hashing anything out between them and she would baulk at any kind of protracted introspection and therapy.

Fox and Freya, the two older children, were also fascinated by Jett, *and* Cato. Though always supervised with them, they were allowed occasionally to hold the two babies. This never lasted for long though: their active minds, now stimulated by the richness of their environment, sent them all over the grounds, where their imagination could rampage, and where they could torment with their curiousness every group member they could find.

The two of them also promptly joined in with the games of barn football. They played it whenever they could and then also when no willing adults were available either. The clean air of the countryside had seemed to clear up all of Freya's ailments, her asthmatic symptoms rarely bothered her and she was free to run and play with her brother as much as she pleased.

Their parents, Max and Jonet, fitted in nicely with the rest of the group. Max had taken an interest in Draven's many engineering and carpentry projects and he assisted him where he could, which Draven appreciated. Jonet had had an idea to keep a diary after Rumer had mentioned to her that Hya had some stationery. She wanted to log their time at the farm with something she and the children might be able to look back on. So she borrowed a pen and one of Hya's notepads and set about writing something, however brief, each day. Though her intention was to record a date for each entry, where the days began and ended soon became indistinguishable. She would have to settle for just the pleasure of doing it.

Draven had been excited since receiving the book from Bodhi at the village and was anxious to read it. During the debrief with Max, Jonet and the others, he kept touching its edges as it sat slotted tantalisingly inside his jacket pocket. He nodded along to the discussion but really he couldn't think about much else.

Since he had relinquished the outbuilding to the new family, he couldn't disturb the others in the barn with torchlight and read the book at night, nor was he particularly partial to reading it in their presence anyway. He wanted privacy.

So it wasn't until after a largely sleepless night of anticipation that he was able to settle somewhere on his own and begin. He chose a spot on the grass, out of sight from the barn, where he could savour the book without distraction. He opened it and thumbed through the first few pages. It was handwritten and in a smart italicised style. He pictured whoever it was writing out the words, the words now in front of him and he felt an intimacy with them. They'd both looked upon the same pages, painstakingly curated and passed inadvertently through time from one to the other.

Draven arrived at the preface, which read as follows.

I have written out for posterity the first hand account of Pallas, who moved to the city just over eighteen years ago. She was able to send me many of the entries of her diary before communication was severed.

Though history may be retold, though it may be reconfigured, distorted or destroyed, the following story will at least remain enshrined in perpetuity on the following pages and in the minds of those who read them.

Draven then peeled over another page, and in the centre appeared a title.

18 YEARS IN LOCKDOWN
DIARY (Excerpts)

He turned over again and came to a body of text. He pressed down over the paper, made himself comfortable on the grass and adjusted his blanket, acting as a pillow, behind his head. He marinated for a final moment, then began.

7
DRAVEN READS 18 YEARS IN LOCKDOWN

YEAR 1

DAY 2
I arrived in the city yesterday. It's so different to what I'm used to. But I have a view of the park from my window, so at least that's something green to look at.

DAY 4
I've come at a volatile time: there were further demonstrations in the city centre yesterday. They were protesting the planned perimeter. Things got out of hand. The police arrived and someone was injured.

DAY 7
The protests have continued for many days now, images and video from them are everywhere. The protesters had been fighting the police, some buildings were even set on fire.

DAY 8
A death was reported today. A young woman, who was on her way home, had been caught in the crossfire and a rioter had struck her down. There was public outcry.

DAY 9
The city addressed the incident: they had no option but to send in police reinforcements. They promised to bring back order and make the streets safe again.

DAY 14
I went for a walk in the park today, the first time in a while. It was oddly quiet outside and I wondered if the rioting had put people off going out.

DAY 22
The reinforcements were sent in today. People were coining them the safety team.

DAY 27
Footage was appearing everywhere of clashes between the rioters and the safeties. It was oddly exciting; it's so easy to get swept up in all of this.

DAY 29
It felt very real today as more deaths had been announced from the fighting. Seven had died so far.

DAY 30
I haven't been outside for a while now, I'm rather scared to be honest. They said the fighting could be going on anywhere and it's not advised to go out at the moment.

DAY 32
The city made an announcement today. Lasting for two weeks, there would be a temporary safety lockdown. We would have to stay indoors. I spend most of my time at home anyway, so it doesn't bother me much.

DAY 37
A few days have passed in lockdown. It would be nice to go outside, but I guess I shouldn't feel sorry for myself; I'm lucky, I work from home and I can get everything I need still sent to me. I'm sure there are others in far worse situations than me.

DAY 43
The two weeks are nearly up and I can't wait to go to the park. Though from everything I'm seeing and reading online, I can't help but feel the lockdown might be ending prematurely.

DAY 44
The city announced an extension to the lockdown today, it would continue for another month. It seems like a long time to be inside, but from what they say, we have no other choice.

DAY 51
The fighting continues and seems to be getting worse, the rioters are recruiting new members. The death toll was announced at fifty seven today, from only twenty five yesterday.

DAY 58
The experts were predicting the worst if lockdown was lifted at the end of the month. They were estimating a hundred times the losses if civilians were allowed back onto the streets.

DAY 73
The month has nearly ended and the inevitable announcement came today: the city would go into an indefinite lockdown. They thanked us for our cooperation and said we just needed to keep it up for a little longer.

DAY 74
I haven't been able to work for nearly two months now, so I was relieved to hear they've introduced a basic income for everyone affected. It seems too good to be true really, to be able to sit at home all day, do nothing and get paid for it. I guess lockdown is not that bad after all!

DAY 75
I've been noticing how often I check my phone these days, I just don't want to miss anything, it's addictive. This all feels rather important somehow and I'm actually a part of it.

DAY 87
Some civilians were seen outside today, breaking the rules. There was a video of them which went viral. How could they do such a thing? It was so selfish. They were ruining this for the rest of us.

DAY 174
I've found myself really missing the outside these passed few days. I look out over the park and it's completely empty. I miss the sound of people.

DAY 246
I read an article today, shared with me by a colleague. It was called: *10 Things To Keep You Busy During Lockdown*. Funnily enough, number five was to start a diary, so I've got that one covered at least.

DAY 265
My first basic income came today. I did some shopping, bought some new clothes I liked; I can send them back if they don't fit. The big online stores seem to be running as usual, deliveries haven't been interrupted.

DAY 271
I felt rather down today, and tired. I know I shouldn't complain but it can be hard sometimes, all this time stuck inside. I know they're just keeping us safe and doing what's best for us, and I'm grateful, but when will this actually end?

DAY 334
Reports said the rioters were winning, they were beginning to take over the whole city. The safeties were in retreat.

DAY 353
More measures were announced today for our safety during the fighting. The doorways and windows of all residential buildings would have protective boarding put over them, protecting those inside. No area was safe now from the rioters — though there hadn't been any disturbance around here yet.

YEAR 2

DAY 383
Two safeties came today in their full riot gear. They boarded over the whole building. I can't even see out of my window any more. I can't see the park...nothing!

DAY 385
I really can't get used to this, it just seems so dark and gloomy all the time now; barely any light coming in from outside.

DAY 417
Sometimes I forget I actually used to have a window. It never even occurs to me to look outside any more.

DAY 432
Two more safeties came today, I'm not sure if it was the same two. They came without warning this time. I asked them what they were doing and they said they were here to help the community and it was for our own good. They were putting signs up around the building. They put one on the inside of my apartment door and one on the outside. The inside one read: STAY SAFE. STAY INSIDE. STAY IN YOUR ROOM. FOR YOUR OWN SAFETY AND THE SAFETY OF OTHERS.

DAY 445
I didn't think I ever would but I'm actually missing home today. I haven't spoken to any of them since I moved. I didn't leave on good terms but now I think about them a lot.

DAY 533
Reports from the front line said the safeties were beginning to turn the tide, the treasonists were finally being pushed back. They said it was because of all our hard work; our sacrifice was finally paying off. Just one more big push they said, and everything would soon go back...
...back to norm...
...back...

Draven felt his eyes closing.

...back to normal.

DAY...
...DAY 5...

The writing on the page was starting to blur. He couldn't make it out.

DAY 572
There was...
...there...
...the...

Draven gave up, he couldn't stay awake. He needed some sleep. He would read the rest later.
He felt the cold and got to his feet, picking the book up with him and the blanket. He went back to the barn briskly, trying to warm up. As he walked, he slid the book back into his jacket pocket, he was not quite ready to share it with the others just yet.

8
DRAVEN RETURNS TO THE VILLAGE

Later that day, Draven went to the outhouse, having checked with the new family if he could use it for some writing. It was now too cold to sit outside but he still wanted peace and quiet to finish his book. So he settled down once more, laying his blanket over the floor this time. He took the book from his jacket pocket, thumbed through to where he had left off and continued.

DAY 572
There was a new announcement from the city today. The over seventies would be moved from the city proper to the outskirts. There, they would be looked after in what they were calling care houses. These had been especially made for them. The older population were the most vulnerable and this would get them away from the most dangerous parts of the city. The announcement seemed to be met positively, people were saying it was the considerate thing to do. I spared a thought for the families that would be broken up over this.

DAY 623
There was another incident in the city today, it was all over the news and social media as usual. The city government building had been attacked. There were several deaths and many injured, including civilians. They said the reason it happened was because there weren't enough guards to protect it.

DAY 627
They announced today there would be a draft for the safety team. I suppose that meant anyone could be conscripted, any of us could become a guard! The conscription would take place in one week and a thousand new recruits would be chosen from the civilian database. They would be trained and would join the

safeties to fight for the city. There would be perks too for those chosen.

DAY 634
The draft was today and I wasn't picked, thankfully. They said there would be another one if they ever needed more recruits.

YEAR 3

DAY 780
My city allowance came today, I did some online shopping for some things for the apartment. They have a special delivery team now, which is run by the city itself. It's very efficient. For some goods, they've even started using drones to delivery them. It makes it so much easier.

DAY 824
Some of the treasonists were seen outside the city today, this was the first time they had gone beyond the perimeter. I immediately worried for home, it wasn't *that* far out.

DAY 831
There has been much discussion about those living outside the city and what should be done with them, they were no longer safe with those sightings of the treasonists. They needed the city's help, they couldn't manage the threat on their own.

DAY 847
The decision was finally made today; they had no choice; the outsiders would be moved into the city. They would be much safer here.

DAY 848
Further to the announcement yesterday, the city outlined how the move would work. There wasn't enough housing for the new arrivals, so all dwellings in the city would be divided up, providing the necessary accommodation. The smaller apartments would be

called units, and everyone would be assigned one. I just can't imagine my flat being split up, it's small enough as it is!

DAY 910
The safeties arrived again in the morning, a whole team of them this time. They set about reconstructing the whole interior of my building.

DAY 914
It didn't take them long. It was like a building site for four days but they cleared up and left today. My flat has been completely split in two. A new kitchenette and small bathroom were added to the other section. When they left, they said I could pick which unit to have as I was already here. So I chose the half with the original kitchen and bathroom and they registered me. It feels so cramped now.

DAY 920
The first of the outsiders arrived today. There was an interview with a woman who had arrived with her family. The video was everywhere. *Thank you*, she said to camera, *our city has saved us, saved me and my family. We will do whatever we can to make it up to them for what they have done for us. The people of the city, we are so grateful for your help. We're all in this together and it's everyone's responsibility to do whatever we can. Stay safe and thank you.*

DAY 940
They have been arriving in their droves from the outside for the last week or so. My new neighbour moved in today. I can just about hear him in the unit next to me.

DAY 1117
The city announced today that resources were running low due to the defence efforts. They had no choice but to cut back on supplies. Food would have to be rationed and some foods wouldn't even be available any more. I think I must have put

weight on during lockdown, so this rationing was probably a good thing!

DAY 1211
As I'd expected, there was a further draft for the safeties, they said their numbers were running low again. I wasn't selected this time either. They said the draft would now happen every six months.

YEAR 4

DAY 1468
There were reports today of a new scheme the city was considering going forward with. With our defence still going on, the city was looking to ensure that the same kind of insurgency could never happen again. They were thinking of setting up a new team made up of the younger generation, the under eighteens. That way, they could be trained over many years, they said, and implement new systems that would help build a better future for the city; a future free from revolt.

DAY 1469
More information was released today on the new scheme. It was reported that the city would be recruiting from the ages twelve to eighteen. This would allow enough time for them to be readied for their roles in the future. They would be selected from the database as before. They said they'd be given a better life and a unique opportunity to do something for the good of all of us.

DAY 1500
A month later the scheme was green lit. I probably shouldn't say this, but I felt very uneasy about it. The idea of taking children away from their parents seemed cruel. But no one seemed to be mentioning this, they were only talking about the violence on the streets and how we had to prevent it all from ever happening again...at any cost! They said the future project was the only way we could get back to normality.

DAY 1792
Today, the recruitment age for the project was lowered to ten.

YEAR 5

DAY 1920
In the city update today, they thanked us again for all our hard work and called us heroes for what we were doing. They said finally an end was in sight; the traitors were losing and they would soon be expelled from the city for good.

DAY 2102
For all our efforts, the city announced they would reward us. They were calling it the families program and it would allow people to see their elderly relatives in the care houses on the outskirts. They could visit them in person once every year. Safe travel would be provided and for everyone's benefit, participants must provide a valid reason for going. At least this was something.

YEAR 6

DAY 2471
As the situation in the city was gradually improving, the media attention was turning back to matters on the outside. More traitors had been spotted near the perimeter. The experts were saying more needed to be done, there wasn't enough to stop them breaching the city limits and putting everyone in danger.

DAY 2477
A proposal was being considered to build a new protective barrier around the entire perimeter of the city, guards would even be stationed along it. This would replace the old fencing, which had caused so much controversy in the first place. The new barrier would stop anyone from entering.

DAY 2498
The perimeter proposal was officially approved today. Construction would soon go ahead.

YEAR 7

DAY 2852
It was announced the perimeter was completed today; finished in under a year! They were saying no one could get through it. There was a celebratory air online: people were relieved, they could relax now that there was no possibility of more traitors coming in. People were feeling safe again.

YEAR 9

DAY 3355
The safeties came back today once again. I asked them what they were doing and they didn't even bother replying this time. They took everything from my unit, completely cleared it out! I had no idea what was going on. I shouted at them. All they said was that the materials were needed for the defence effort. I tried to argue but they said if I didn't accept it, I would lose my basic income and maybe even my rations. I kept quiet and they left. I looked around and all I had now was just my bed and my phone.

YEAR 10

DAY 3762
Nothing seems to be changing. I keep checking my phone and there is just opinion pieces, but never any new announcements. I start to wonder if there will ever be an end to this.

YEAR 11

DAY 4196
I keep scrolling, but all there is is articles and conjecture, still never any progress. Everyone loves talking about it, it seems to give them something to do, some meaning in their lives. I see

video after video of all the pundits speculating and all the TV experts talking. They seem to love playing God. It keeps me intrigued enough to keep watching but never motivates me enough to do anything. My faculty for thought has gone, replaced by whatever they tell me to think each day. All I do is follow the story, there's nothing else to do.

YEAR 12

DAY 4432
It's never going to end, is it? I know that now. There's always been risks but now they've taken away my choice to take them. But I trust our city, I do. It knows me, it knows what's best for me. Our city will protect us, it will keep us safe. All we have to do is just whatever it tells us.

YEAR 14

DAY 5114
I thought about this today... I'm a burden, really, aren't I? I mean, I don't contribute any more, I'm just a drain on resources. I'm an extra mouth to feed. I'm a waste of energy. Maybe I should do everyone a favour, then I wouldn't be such a burden any more. The future would be much better off without me; one less footprint to worry about.

YEAR 15

DAY 5550 (????)
I won't see you again ever, will I? I wonder what you're doing, were all of you moved to the city? Where are you, I wonder? I should tell you all this, shouldn't I? Some one has to know. Yes, I'll send you all this when I'm done.

YEAR 17

DAY ??????????

I thought today about everything - too much time to think - from the day I moved here, to now, now which is I don't know when... Year 17...I think... Where did it go, all the years? And what did I do but waste them all? Yes, they're all gone now. And what price have I paid for my devotion to this illusion? My time? My life perhaps...? And why? Why did I lend myself to this? My safety? The safety of others? Responsibility: that vague master that controls us? I was tricked by the promise that I would be a good person, that I was doing the right thing. And what did I give just to seem considerate, to appear virtuous, to be judged well in the minds of those trapped in delirium and fever? I knelt for acceptance in the eyes of the judgemental, convinced of and by their own superiority. They were so certain, and so angry, and it was this madness of mobs that compelled me. In their wrath, I complied. For them, for the city, for the future, I handed over my sovereignty. Was my sacrifice worth it? Did it even count? I came here, to this city, with a life ahead of me, with dreams in my heart and ambition in my head. Now my life is behind me. And I spent it doing what? Watching the stories of others, and the supposed biggest story of them all play out. I have no stories of my own, nothing to tell. I am but a cog, a number to document, a statistic to discuss. I am insignificant.

YEAR 18?

I will. I will tomorrow, tomorrow, I will... And that will be that. For the future...it's better off without me...

Pallas

END

Draven's eyes filled with tears. His emotions consumed him and he felt he might break down and sob. He stopped himself and held on tightly to what he was feeling; he didn't want the relief of crying. For just a little while longer, he wanted to keep his tears, for his tears might carry his emotions away, and he couldn't have his emotions disappear or fall to the ground to be trodden on. He needed the anguish to stay.

He mourned for some time, reflecting on what he had read. He *was* Pallas, he thought, all of them were Pallas, and all those still in the city were Pallas. Each had had a life stolen from them. They were never given any choice.

He looked up from the book, hearing laughter and chatter coming from outside. The barn and the field had come back to life. Draven appreciated the group more now than he ever had. He wanted desperately to see them prosper and to grow and he would do whatever he could to help them. But he knew they were outgrowing the farm, it was small and the barn cramped, and a chastening winter would soon be upon them. It would test them unbearably and perhaps irrevocably again.

But there was something else Draven knew he could do.

He kept true to his word and returned to the village in the early days of winter when he still could. In the relative comfort of the church, he and Bodhi spoke of Pallas's story and a considerable time passed unnoticed by them. When their philosophical meanderings came to an end, Draven told Bodhi that he knew it was him who penned the book. Not least because it could have only *been* him given the time frame, but there was a more ethereal reason too: the book had retained some fabric that Draven recognised of its creator.

He had just one more question of Bodhi to complete the puzzle.

'So who is Pallas?' he said, 'Is she real?'

'Yes, of course she's real,' Bodhi answered, almost sounding offended, 'Pallas is my sister,' he declared.

With this, Draven mentally connected the last few pieces. Pallas had left for the city when they were young and eighteen years later, perhaps as her last action, had sent him her diary entries, unlikely ever knowing if he'd received them. From these, Bodhi had created the book, writing up all the entries he had and placing the finished book in the safest place he knew; at the back of the church. He had wanted Draven to read it above anything else so had handed it to him on their visit. But he didn't want to colour it with his own involvement and so only said that a former villager had written it. When Bodhi had spoken of loss, it was likely his sister's leaving that most afflicted him, and when he had advised Draven about the hourglass, it would have been mostly informed by how much he had missed *her*.

'When she left for the city,' Bodhi explained, 'We didn't part on good terms. We didn't speak. But then, I started receiving messages from her years and years later, just before they cut communication with the outside. It was her diary. And I'm sure you noticed, not all of it came through, especially the later years, but she obviously wanted someone to see it. I wrote up everything I could, I had to do that for her. It had to be documented somewhere at least.'

Then Bodhi leant in closer to Draven and emoted his next words very uncharacteristically, almost aggressively.

'This is her story,' he said, 'And I won't see it messed around with by some click of someone's button.'

Empathetically, Draven then spoke of Ophelia and Caius, his old friends he had lost over a fatal winter. Bodhi had been right about him and it was *they* who he had been grieving for. He told Bodhi that his advice, especially visualising the hourglass as empty, had helped him come to terms with their passing.

After much discussion, they finally left the church. But just before Draven departed he asked something else of Bodhi. Bodhi agreed to his proposal and after heartfelt valedictions, Draven left for the farm.

Upon his return, Draven gathered the group. He explained to them what many of them were already thinking; there were now too many of them to stay here. He also questioned their resilience in an unsheltered barn to another winter, especially with them now seldom risking open fires. Everyone nodded in agreement. He told them that a man they'd met on excursion had invited them to live in his village, keeping it to himself that *he'd* actually been the one to ask on their behalf. He described the stone buildings there that would keep them warm and that there were enough houses that each of them could have their own. The others who had been there; Annia, Otto and Jago, concurred and were also full of approbation for it.

Draven then revealed the book from his pocket and held it out as if it crowned his pitch. The others looked at it in wonder. He said to them there would be a whole library of books waiting for them at the village.

With the testimony of all those who had seen it, the others were convinced and the matter was settled: the group would move to the village. They packed their bags that night, leaving a few supplies there for any return, and the next day, they left for their new home.

6
THE VILLAGE

1
ENGAGEMENT

The winter passed, this time without event. The village was far more habitable than the farm and the sturdy construct of their houses shielded the group from the inclemency of the season. They spent most of their days inside, having hoarded what food and water they could before the most inhospitable weeks arrived.

The group mostly separated into their pairings when they'd arrived, each choosing a house to live in. Firstly, next to the church was the rectory, where Jago, Amica and their child Cato, resided. Amica was now pregnant with a second and with the rectory one of the largest buildings in the village, it would allow them room to grow. Next door to them, were Ever, Cleo and *their* son, Jett. Opposite and a little further along the main pathway, were Rumer and Hya. Along from them, was the family of Max, Jonet and their two children, Fox and Freya. Then, the ones who had chosen to live alone; in the set of houses off the street from the main square, was Otto. He was next door to Annia. Opposite them, was Draven. And lastly, next door but one to him, was Bodhi, who was still living in his childhood home. He and his close neighbour Draven formed a strong companionship over the winter, often visiting one another when they could. When spring arrived, Draven, who had always hiked alone, now had someone accompanying him.

As the ides of spring came and went, one afternoon, Cleo and Ever requested the company of the others to join them in the village square, which had become the group's customary meeting place. Habitually, the group sat in their usual places, on benches or on rugs on the ground, then waited for Cleo and Ever to speak.

Ever took a deep breath and it was obvious to the others this was something he had rehearsed.

'We can't thank everyone enough for all your help,' he began, slowly and deliberately, 'If it wasn't for all of you, we would've never met each other, and we wouldn't be here now of course.'

He steadied himself and considered his next line carefully.

'So, Cleo and I have been together for a while now and...,' he turned to the church and raised a hand towards it, '...we want to get married.'

He smiled at the group.

There was a pause as the news sunk in amongst them.

Ever appeared to have already finished.

'*Married*?' Otto scoffed.

'Yes, married,' confirmed Cleo.

'But, no one's been married for...what, nearly fifteen years,' remarked Annia.

'So all the more reason.'

There was another pause.

Then Hya blurted out, 'What's the point?'

At this, a few hushed chuckles precipitated around the group. They weren't sure if they should laugh, so they checked Cleo and Ever's reaction. They looked rather stunned.

'Say what you mean, Hya,' Otto said jokingly, standing next to her, 'Don't feel you need to sugar coat it.'

There was more subdued laughter.

Hya could feel the accusation of the group and felt she needed to explain.

'Well, it's just a waste of time, isn't it... I mean, you already have a child, everyone here knows you're together and it doesn't mean anything any more anyway.'

Cleo and Ever looked dumbstricken back at her. They had imagined quite a different reaction to their announcement.

Then, to the group's surprise, Bodhi stood up, he was the last person they'd expected to speak.

'It's not a waste of time,' he said, as calmly as ever, 'Even if we do all know about it. And I think perhaps, it's more important now than its ever been actually. I think it's wonderful that they want to affirm their love outwardly, in front of us all.'

Hya shot Bodhi a challenging glare.

'Well, I wish they'd do it inwardly,' she came back, 'But seriously, why do it? It's just showing off, isn't it? It's just saying, look how great a couple we are to other people. No one cares how great a couple you are. Face it, people only have weddings so a bunch of friends have to tell them how good they look. It's just vanity.'

There was a disconcerting silence, the rest of the group were unclear whether they should be finding this all amusing or not.

'So…anyway…,' Otto said, ridiculing the awkwardness. He always enjoyed mocking Hya's occasional clumsy outspokenness.

Hya then caught a glimpse of Rumer next to her, she had her head buried in her hands, looking like she was trying to hide from the whole situation! Hya realised her comments may have been rooted in her and Rumer's current relationship difficulties. She realised she was jealous of Ever and Cleo.

Bodhi rejoined over a murmur of laughter.

'They're not doing it for themselves,' he said, 'they're doing it for the group. Ever started by saying they wanted to thank us. So it's not *their* wedding at all, it's *our* wedding. It's a celebration for all of us.'

Otto quickly bouldered in again.

'Yes, why do you have to be such a grinch, Hya.'

He was deliberately provoking her, a cheeky grin appearing over his face.

Hya stood up, turned and thwacked Otto on the arm, though at least partially in jest. He recoiled comedically, clutching his arm. The group burst out laughing at their play acting, seeing the theatrics as their permission to laugh openly at last. Even Hya saw the funny side, a half smile turning up her lips. Cleo and Ever perked up too, seeming impervious to any aspersions, they were visibly amused now.

The group slowly settled down and Hya felt the onus on her once again to say something.

'Look, fine, I just think it's a bit of a waste,' she said, 'But sure, if it makes you happy, why not…' Then she added in her own attempt at light heartedness, 'Maybe you can get your divorce here too.'

At this, there was more laughter.
Cleo spoke over it.
'Well, I think I've found my chief bridesmaid.'

2
THE PRAIRIES BY THE VILLAGE

She could feel Hya breathing, her head gently undulating on her stomach, a muted thump of a heart just above. But that was all Rumer could hear from her, the two of them weren't speaking. Summer was upon the group and they were enjoying their indolence. Hya and Rumer had walked to the fields in silence, as they were now. They lay how they were, with Rumer rested on Hya, but only routinely; the troubles between them had only festered as they continued to ignore them.

They had invited Maxen and Jonet to join them — their children, Fox and Freya, were still playing. The couple had been asked under the guise of taking in the wonderful sunset from the prairies, though they were really asked so that Hya and Rumer wouldn't be alone; alone, they might have to confront their problems, which they'd rather not do. But the romantic overtones of the scene had prised the older couple away from them a short distance. So with their ruse unsuccessful, Rumer and Hya *were* alone and the air was uncomfortable between them.

'So you wouldn't want us to get married then?' Rumer needled, her words laced with thorny disapproval.

'No,' came a punctuated response.

Rumer's head was still rested on Hya's torso. Undeterred, she probed further.

'Why not?'

'What's wrong with what we have?' Hya negotiated.

'I just don't think marriage is showing off, it's a way of professing feelings, solidifying them. And guests are witnesses, not some kind of accessory like you make out. They are supposed to help the couple uphold their vows in the future, that's why they're there.'

There was no rebuttal.

'I just miss the old Hya,' she added.

At this, Hya cavilled.

'Who's the old Hya?' she snapped, then not allowing Rumer redress, added, 'It's a childish thing to say, *the old Hya*. What does that even mean?'

'It's not childish,' Rumer retorted, 'I mean, the Hya who used to confide in me, who was joky, and passionate, and kind, and… The Hya who I met in the letters…'

'I wonder who the Hya she met in the letters was…?' Max said with a wry grin.

Max and Jonet could overhear the other conversation as their voices elevated.

Jonet couldn't help but smile back, despite feeling they were prying.

'I don't know, maybe it's someone we haven't met yet,' she contributed, not being able to resist joining in.

They laughed and the rush of gaiety caused Jonet to roll over onto Max's front and they kissed impulsively in a manner they hadn't for many years. The setting and their silliness had intoxicated them.

The two of them were approaching forty and they felt eminently qualified to judge the fledgling couple lying over from them. Though *their* youthful machismo was all but gone, it was perhaps this reminder of it from the tempestuous lovers opposite that had caused Jonet and Max to feel so unusually amorous.

Hya sighed, pushing herself to consider Rumer's point of view: perhaps *there was* something to what she'd said.

Writing had always been cathartic for Hya, a way to release emotions she might otherwise withhold. Living in the city had hardened her and engendered a coldness. It was only when she wrote she felt she could be open, congenial, and even sentimental. She reserved a separate persona for the page which was quite different from how she was away from it.

Rumer had recognised this duality in her. She had been initially attracted to Hya through their letter correspondence and so to the traits of hers she usually kept hidden. But this more guarded, intransigent Hya she'd known since the underground, could sometimes be trying.

'I never stopped writing, you know,' Hya said after an extended pause, 'During the raids, when they took our stuff, I managed to hide a few things from them. My stationery for one... So I would write, write more than I ever did before.'

Rumer came up off Hya and sat herself up so she could see her face.

'Writing was therapeutic for me,' Hya went on, 'I couldn't express myself otherwise. I could never articulate exactly what I wanted to say, so I wrote it down. There was something about the permanence of the pen and paper, the mark on the page, it's like an inscription, a statement that you have to stand behind. You can't change it.'

Hya, who had so far only stared out over the horizon, looked at Rumer for the first time that evening. As their eyes met, this alone was enough for them to feel a level of intimacy they hadn't for some time.

The negativity lifted.

Hya's face then slowly creased over as she cracked a smile.

'So, you think I'm better on paper then?' she said deviously.

Rumer didn't smile, too concerned Hya had taken her criticisms to heart.

'No, no,' she pleaded, 'I didn't mean that. I just meant a little bit of the old Hya would be nice. I like you as you are, really, but just a tiny bit, a tiny bit of the old Hya, that's all.'

She then *did* offer her own smile too.

Hya then quipped, 'Well, I made a joke. That's a good start, right.'

'Right, it is. Thanks.'

Rumer lay her head back down onto Hya and pecked her stomach.

They continued to watch the now dwindling sunset.

Jonet and Max found themselves eaves dropping again, Hya's compelling insight hushing them. Her words were captivating and they needed to remind themselves it was Hya being so loquacious.

Jonet propped herself up as Rumer had, her and Max were now eye to eye.

'We should get some books from Bodhi,' she said, inspired by what they'd just heard, 'It might help me with my diary writing too.'

'Oh yeah, definitely,' Max agreed, '...Real books, huh? It's unimaginable, isn't it?'

'I know, and neither of us have even bothered to visit the library yet.'

Max mentally counted. 'I don't think I've read a book for nearly twenty years.'

Jonet smiled, then cosied up to him, putting her arms around his waist.

The cooler evening air started to paint their skin. Max took a blanket from their bag and draped it over them as they entangled themselves even closer. They watched as the red glow descended beyond the contours of the hills; the great firmament of the sky disappearing from their laic sight. Finally, there was not a trace left of the outline of the land, not a shape, nor shadow.

Max and Jonet got up, wished the others good night and headed back to the village, leaving Rumer and Hya be. They came to the square where the kids were still playing, even though they could barely still see. They took them home and put them to bed, retiring themselves shortly after. They couldn't have imagined such simplicity could fulfil them so completely.

Elsewhere that night, and making the most of an idyllic summer's day, Otto and Annia had taken a walk along the river. With the upheaval moving to the village and the new faces bedding in, as something of ambassadors for the group, they felt the pressure to welcome the newbies and be cordial, and this was an effort for both of them. At least alone and away from the others, they could laugh, joke and frolic as they wished. There was no need to have to try with each other.

They had stopped by the riverbed and were looking out over the peaceful water.

Otto spoke after some time had passed.

'I guess we're pretty much together now then.'

Annia remained silent, leaving enough of a pause to incline Otto to elaborate. He did.

'I think we should just tell everyone. Get it out in the open, they already know anyway really.'

'I agree,' Annia responded, 'It's annoying having to dance around it in front of them.'

'Okay,' confirmed Otto. He paused, then spoke again, 'And...there's one more thing...'

He turned to face her.

'I think we should live together too,' he proposed, 'We're next door anyway. It makes sense.'

She thought about it in her pragmatic way.

'Yes,' she said, turning to him, 'That does make sense.'

Otto gave a half smile. She reciprocated.

And so business seemed to have already been concluded between them.

Then, as if contrived perfectly, they embraced romantically with the river as their background and the scorched water from the setting sun silhouetting them rather epically.

3
THE WEDDING

At the height of summer, with the warmth unabated, Cleo and Ever married. The bucolic scene of yesteryear, with the church, and surrounded by the village, delighted the group. Though a few of them had attended weddings online, only Draven had been to one in person. Jonet and Max, married themselves, were one of the last couples to wed online. The practice was deemed obsolete soon after, then outlawed outright by the city. So the group were over the moon to have the opportunity for such an experience.

The event was simple. The group hadn't many decorations and so the church was dressed minimally, only a bloom of summer flowers they had picked from the wild strewn along the aisle. The rest of the church was swept and cleaned so the wood and the stone were smart and polished. There was little else the group could add, but they felt it was left to look beautifully understated.

There were few outfits to choose from for them, only the clothes each had brought with them and a few garments they had fixed together from materials they had found. Ever wore the same jeans he'd left the city in and a borrowed shirt from Bodhi. He had added a waistcoat fashioned from a rectangular strip of cloth with two arm holes cut out of it. It was not shapely but the patchwork outfit seemed to compliment Ever's rakish charm nevertheless. Cleo wore a linen dress, also made from material they'd found, it was plainly cut and strapless. Her entourage had wrapped it around her and fixed it together at the back so it would stay in place. It too was unbecoming, but similarly played to *her* folksiness; the whimsical look reminding the group the brio she inspirited in them. Both also attended bare foot, only each having one pair of shoes, and those were for hiking. This, likewise, just served the dilettantish vibes and laid back nature of their event.

The guests were equally sartorially unaccomplished, but they added what regalia and fripperies they could to their everyday outfits. Leaves had been collected from the woods, folded and interlaced into patterns to create decorations. The group tied these to their tops as lapel pins or slotted them into their hair.

The motley congregation organised themselves onto the pews in the nave. Ever waited with Otto at the front of the chancel. Bodhi stood beyond them and was to assume the sacerdotal duties conducting the ceremony. Jago, Amica, Cato, Jett and Annia sat on one side of the aisle, while Max, Jonet, Fox, Freya, Draven and Rumer sat on the other. Cleo had carried through on her jocular remark that Hya should be her chief bridesmaid, and Hya, though reluctantly, had come good, feeling she ought to.

So Cleo walked down the aisle, Hya alongside her. Rumer smiled and Ever grinned. Fox bore rings to Bodhi, and Freya brought a bouquet to Cleo. The rings were formed of tightly twisted hay, symbolically taken from the barn at the group's first settlement. Once they had exchanged rings, they started to irritate the skin on their fingers. They hadn't foreseen this but neither let it bother them.

As the ceremony neared its end, the children became irritable themselves. Baby Jett was the one exception coincidentally; obviously realising the importance of his parent's matrimony. Freya had started making random noises and was soon reproved by Max, Fox audibly sulked at having to be still for so long and was quickly placated by Jonet, and Cato, who'd started to cry, was taken outside the church entirely by Amica. Bodhi, seen as something of a spiritual presence among the group, was patient with the children and waited for them to tire themselves somewhat and for Amica and Cato to come back inside.

He had crafted a well paced and dignified service for the couple and he had come to his final benediction. In his preparedness, he had gone to the lengths of searching the sacristy for an old Bible and had found a reading he felt appropriate for the occasion. He waited for peace to descend, then he began.

> *'Each will be like a hiding place from the wind,*
> *a covert from the tempest,*
> *like streams of water in a dry place,*
> *like the shade of a great rock in a weary land.*
>
> *'The populous city deserted,*
> *the hill and the watchtower will become dens forever.*
> *Until the wilderness becomes a fruitful field,*
> *and the fruitful field is deemed a forest.*
>
> *'Then justice will dwell in the wilderness,*
> *and righteousness abide in the fruitful field.*
> *The effect of righteousness will be peace,*
> *and the result of righteousness, quietness and trust forever.*
>
> *'My people will abide in a peaceful habitation,*
> *in secure dwellings, and in quiet resting places.*
> *The city will be utterly laid low.*
> *Happy will you be who sow beside every stream.'*

Bodhi took a moment and then looked up to see the grateful faces of the group. He had been cautious about them coming to the village, worried they would rekindle old feelings that he had carefully suppressed. He had forgotten the outside world by intention but now he longed again for companionship and family. And in that moment as he looked at the group, he thought he had found them. The hurt he might endure if he lost them paled to the feeling of belonging he had now.

After his peroration, Bodhi prompted Ever and Cleo to kiss and the rest clapped in honour of their union. Ever collected baby Jett from Annia, rejoined Cleo, and with interlocking arms, they recessed back down the aisle, as petals were thrown over them. The rest gradually paraded from the church behind them and the group reconvened outside for further celebration.

The dogs were waiting there to congratulate them and the group socialised in the village square for the rest of the afternoon. They drank and ate merrily. They laughed and smiled and embraced each other zealously. The floor became adorned with the leaf designs that fell from their clothing and out from their hair. Their outfits started to unravel as they cavorted on the gravel and the group soon looked more bedraggled than they ever had before.

As the afternoon wore on, the group began to lounge about lackadaisically into a keen summer's evening. They chatted, enjoyed each other's company and were only interested in one another. Blissfully undistracted and unconcerned with anything else, they relaxed in joyful amity.

The kids; Fox and Freya, broke off from the main group around the square. They were bored of the adult company and had started another game of barn football — though now not against a barn but the side of an unoccupied house.

Jago looked over at them as they kicked the ball back and forth from the wall. Then, he saw another figure emerge, stumbling and toddling towards the other two. A tiny figure. It was Cato.

Jago went to get him but then paused to watch. Cato could hardly stand but the ball happened to roll to him. He kicked it with all his might, nearly falling over under his own momentum. The ball rolled slowly, painstakingly towards the side of the house. Jago could see each rotation as it crept inch by inch closer. Then, as it stopped still, it managed to just brush up against the wall.

Fox and Freya leapt for joy at seeing it and screamed at the top of their voices in adulation. They rushed over to Cato, hugged each side of him and lifted him into the air. They spun him and cheered wildly for him. Jago could see Cato's confused but seemingly contented face. A few of the others then came to rescue him from the overbearing and overeager siblings. But not before they also congratulated him on his big achievement.

Jago sat back into his chair, where memories rushed back to him of his *own* childhood again. He saw the fields once more, the football, the graze on his knee, and the sun in the sky. Then he looked back at Cato and it was no longer himself he saw in those fields, but his son. He and Amica were by his side. And that was all he could see.

4
MAXEN GOES TO THE QUARRY

'Your first time out?' Otto said to Max.

'Yes,' Max replied.

The two of them were preparing their bags. Now in late summer, and armed with report of a quarry to the west, a small group of them were setting off in search of it. Draven, having discovered the site with Bodhi on one of their long peregrinations, was going with them to see what useful materials he could find there. Otto and Hya would go too, as they usually did, but a fourth and debuting member was also tagging along.

For the time he had been with them, Max had been fascinated with Draven's endeavours; he would watch as he transformed innocuous looking trash into tools, farming equipment and even furnishings for the houses. Having repurposed one of the available buildings, Draven had a much larger studio now and Max had begun to help him where he could. The trip would be an opportunity for Max to learn more about what materials Draven used and how he sourced them.

'Well, it's about a two day hike,' Otto continued, 'Draven thought he saw some old machinery he could use, you know, for all his crazy stuff.' He lifted his bag onto his shoulders. 'So, ready to check it out?'

'Sounds good,' Max said, hoping he sounded suitably eager.

'That's the spirit,' Otto said manfully, 'You'll fit right in,' then he patted Max firmly on the back.

Max responded in kind, supposing it a kind of fraternal gesture.

'Where's Annia anyway?' he said, 'She usually comes, no?'

'*Annia*?' Otto replied.

'Yes, Annia,' Max repeated, 'Didn't you two just…move… Aren't…you two… together…?'

'I'd say together's a bit strong.'

'Oh, didn't you say —'

'Not really sure where she is,' Otto cut Max off, 'Think she said she's not feeling well or something…,' he said, pretending to be nonplussed.

'Oh okay, fair enough,' Max said, sensing he should probably move on.

Otto turned back to the square.

'Hya, Draven, you ready already?' he shouted at them.

They were also finishing packing a little away from them.

'Yes, coming,' Hya shouted back.

Rumer woke in their room, Hya had already left for the quarry. Rumer sat up against the wall, plumped her pillow and put it behind her. She pulled her knees up towards her chest, then pulled the blanket up over her knees. She reached for her book from the bedside table. On it was a note. It must have been left for her by Hya.

Though Hya had brought her writing materials with her from the city, Rumer had not seen her use them once, despite several others having asked to borrow them. The note on the book was folded over, just like how her letters used to arrive back in their building. It must have been a gesture, she thought, catalysed by their conversation on the prairies and perhaps, in part, from the ardour of the wedding too.

Rumer took it, unfolded it, and this alone triggered memories of when she received her first letter from Hya back in her unit. She had the same feelings of intrigue and excitement, and even some dread resurfaced too, though she quickly rationalised *that* emotion away. What could Hya have put to paper after such a long abeyance? She looked over the letter, the writing was the same, unmistakably Hya's scrawl. Rumer was giddy.

She read on.

Rumer,
I'll be away for a couple of days as you know.
I finally wrote another letter for you, so, well done me, I suppose.

It's not that I don't understand you, I know it must be difficult with someone like me, someone who isn't giving you much to work with. But it's just my way of dealing with things. I hope you can stick by me. I want you to know that I want us to stay together, however tough it gets, or however difficult I can be. I will try. I want us to live in this house - this is our house now - and in our village, with our friends, no matter what, for as long as we are able.

Hyacinth. X

In some ways, Rumer thought, this was a typically *Hya* response: it played to her sentiment and was just enough that she might temporarily forget her frustration, zero her grievance counter and wait for it to count up again. But there was something else in the letter too, something she'd never heard from Hya before; there was a statement of her intent. She'd promised Rumer not only her presence but her commitment for as long as she could, and this was significant.

Rumer immediately felt better, her deepest concern for Hya's investment had been largely ameliorated and her minor gripes now just seemed trivial. Her perspective changed and she thought about the wider circumstance they found themselves. She wondered how she could have possibly allowed herself to be unhappy, how she could have conspired to perceive her world negatively. She realised how fortunate she was, how fortunate all the group were. Her troubles had been exorcised from her body.

Two days later, the out group returned from the quarry. Cleo, Ever and Jett were seated in the square and watched them as they arrived back. As Otto came into view, he dropped his bag and fell to his knees. Draven came up behind him, putting a hand on his shoulder, then sat down next to him. Hya then appeared, walking passed both of them and coming up to where they were sitting.

'Are they okay?' Cleo asked her.

Hya stopped. She didn't answer.

Otto stood up in the distance behind her. He kicked the wall of the churchyard, some stone fragments sprayed over the pathway.

'What's wrong?' Cleo said with new urgency. Jett started to cry, sensing his mother's distress.

'Where's Jonet, Max and Freya?' Hya said sternly, ignoring Cleo's questions.

'I-I think they went for a walk. What's going on, Hya?' Cleo implored.

'Max is dead,' said Hya.

'What?' Ever said, standing up.

Hya was unflinching, she didn't respond. She just turned and stared at the pathway entering the village, where Jonet and the children would likely return.

'No one else say anything,' she said uncompromisingly, 'I will tell them.'

Cleo and Ever managed to nod to her even through their sudden trauma. Cleo stood up too, and placing a brief hand on Hya's shoulder, they both went, with Jett, to check on Draven and Otto. They knew Hya would be shut off now until she could speak to Jonet.

Hya brunted herself with the responsibility of telling Max's family, she felt it her duty. She did not know how the children would even comprehend death, but she had to be the one to tell them. She was most upset for Fox, with whom she had formed an unlikely friendship, and she couldn't bear to think how this might affect him at such an early age. She liked Max, like all the group did, he was a friend, but she couldn't allow *herself* the luxury of grieving; that would be selfish. It was the family's prerogative to mourn, and theirs alone.

Hya didn't change her clothes and she didn't go home. She didn't eat, or drink, she just waited, waited for Jonet and the children to return. She sat in the square and kept watch of the pathway. She was there for the best part of the day and refused to move.

As the others went inside for the evening and Hya was left alone outside, finally she saw the figures of Jonet, Fox and Freya appear in the distance. She stood up immediately and went to them. She dismissed the children to the churchyard and they frittered away.

'Don't be too long,' Jonet said to them and turned to Hya, wondering what was going on.

'You will want to sit,' Hya said formally, and gestured to one of the stone benches.

Jonet sat down and anxiously waited.

Hya crouched down in front of her. She looked at Jonet like a doctor might; dispassionate, passive, and started to speak.

'We were at the quarry yesterday, myself, Otto, Draven and Max. We were looking around when we heard a sound in the sky. Another drone had come. This time, there were two of them. We ran for cover in the woods, separating so we'd be harder to see. They flew passed, I don't think they saw us. We regrouped but couldn't find Max. We searched for him and when we came to the edge of the quarry, we found him. He must have lost his footing whilst running. He had fallen in.'

Hya could see the warmth slowly leaving Jonet's body, her face turning ashen. Hya wanted desperately to squeeze the warmth back into her, but she had to finish.

'We climbed down to him, but there was nothing we could do. He wasn't breathing. He had died from the fall.'

Hya watched what remaining spirit fade from Jonet's eyes.

There was silence.

'Thank you for telling me,' Jonet said simply.

She stood up and walked slowly to the churchyard.

Hya stayed on one knee and watched as Jonet called the two children over and knelt before them. She put her arms around their shoulders and pulled them in. She started speaking. The children looked back wide eyed, then their faces became tearful. Fox, the older sibling wept and Freya looked up at him in confusion; perhaps not understanding the permanence just yet.

Hya couldn't turn away.

She thought of the loss of her own father years ago, how such a presence in her life was gone in an instant; a guiding hand no more, and nothing would be the same again. With wetted eyes, she watched Fox cry in the distance. He was sobbing unashamedly and childishly; he didn't cover his face, he didn't wipe away any tears, but cried openly and in full view. Fox would now have to endure what she had. But she hoped that at least he might be tougher for it. She promised to herself in that moment that she would watch over him as long as she could.

Max's passing affected the group indelibly. They were insensible to the charms of the rest of the summer and the early fall, they hardly socialised and stayed mostly in their houses. The shorter days and the chill of autumn then kept them there. So much so, that the group barely noticed the birth of Djuna, Amica and Jago's second child. The news took many weeks to proliferate, but as it did, the others took their turns to visit the rectory and welcome the latest arrival.

Jago and Amica had mostly stepped back from the leadership they'd always felt incumbent on them. They'd shouldered much of the care of the group since they'd met the others on the farm. But now with the demands of two little ones, they'd decided to minimise their involvement.

With this reclusion over the summer, they now needed to re-familiarise themselves with social behaviour as the others visited them. They found it wearing at first, but through gritted politeness they soon became genuinely pleased to see everyone and grateful for all their interest.

This morning, it was Annia's turn to come and see them.

'How do you find it with them then?' she said, 'It must be tough...'

She was sat next to Amica, who was cradling Djuna. Annia was staring at the baby.

'It can be,' Amica answered, 'But it's certainly a nice environment to bring kids up in. We have the fresh air, warm houses, helpful people around us, what more do we need?'

Jago sat on the other side of the room. Cato crawled between them. Every so often, he came to his feet before bumping back down again.

'Right,' Annia said, still staring at Djuna. 'Is it difficult though, you know, without technology, health wise and all that...you know, looking after them...?'

Amica noticed Annia didn't seem herself. Her mannerisms didn't belong to her and her usual felicitousness was now meandering.

'Er, not really,' Amica replied, 'It's how nature intended, as they say.'

'Who says?' challenged Annia, her eyes for once darting up to Amica.

Amica looked back at a befuddled looking Annia.

'Well, you know,' she said, 'Just people in general say, don't they?'

'Do they?' Annia said, looking away up to the ceiling as she thought about it. 'Oh, right, like a saying,' she added, '*how nature intended*.'

Jago looked up from Cato to the others, also noticing Annia's odd behaviour.

'Yes, like a saying,' Amica confirmed.

Then Amica realised *why* Annia was acting so strangely and all Annia's questioning suddenly made sense.

'Any news you want to share with us?' she asked her leadingly.

Annia ignored this and continued with her enquiries.

'But do you get any time to yourself, to relax or anything?'

'Yes, sometimes,' Jago joined in from across the room, 'If we get a sitter, it means we can get out from time to time,' he glanced at Annia, 'You've sat for us a few times remember…'

'Yes, of course,' she responded. She paused, then added, 'But at this rate, aren't we going to end up with more children than adults?'

At this, Amica and Jago shared a look. Jago had now cottoned on also.

'Well, I suppose that's the general idea really,' replied Amica.

A few moments passed.

'Sure there's nothing you want to tell us?' Amica asked again.

Annia looked away, then back.

'Yes, Otto and I,' she started, 'we're having a child.'

'Aw, that's great,' Amica said, upbeat though feigning her surprise.

'Yes, congratulations,' Jago added, 'I'll congratulate Otto when I see him too.'

'Oh, yeah,' muttered Amica, 'about that. I haven't actually told him yet,' she looked over at Jago, 'I will soon.'

'Oh okay,' said Jago, 'I won't mention it then, don't worry.'

'Yep, we won't say anything,' Amica added.

They both smiled at Annia considerately.

'Thanks,' Annia said, turning her attention back to Djuna once more.

5
AMICA'S REGRET

'I close my eyes and I see them in the sky, and I hear them. I'm running from them, but they're not chasing me, they're chasing you, and Cato, and Djuna. You're running but you can't escape, wherever you go, they're there. Then you fall, you all fall, just like Max did. And I can't save you, I can't save any of you.

'Since he died, I've kept thinking about it. No matter how long ago, and how far away, I still think of the city. It's beating me, it's winning. I don't want it to but it stays with me. And now it's not just me, but it comes for you, the children, and the others too. And it's all my fault.

'The longer I wait, the worse it will get. I need closure, Jago, and I think this is the only way.

'I have to go again, but this time, I won't turn back, I can't. I told you; I left them behind and I chose you instead. That was self centred of me, and now I'm paying for it. I have to go back for them. I have to help them. It's the only way.

'Can you understand?'

Jago and Amica were sat alone on the benches in the church.

Jago was reminded of the conversation they'd had just before the last time Amica had left for the city. He had been expecting it again now Djuna was born. He knew that Max's death had impacted her and she would blame herself for what had happened, whether the drones had come for her or not. She had retrogressed and her mind was once again populated with thoughts of the city. She couldn't forget it and her only path to redemption was to return for the others she once knew. That was the salvation she craved.

'I can,' said Jago, quiet and laconic.

There was a stillness in the church. Not even the whistles of wind through the cracks in the stone could disturb it.

Jago spoke again after a prolonged silence.

'What is your plan?'

Amica sighed. 'The same. No reason it should change. But I'm going to warn them this time, so they can be ready. We won't have to go to them, they'll come to us.'

Jago frowned, 'How?'

'My phone, it's still in the car in the woods. It should be close enough to the city for a signal. So I'm going to message them.'

'And it will still work?'

'If it turns on, yes, don't see why it shouldn't.'

Though Jago, as he always would, hated the idea of Amica returning to the city, he too, like all the others, had been affected heavily by Max's death. It had roused a bellicosity in him that had been shelved during their domesticity in the village. Jago found he was now far less objectionable this time to Amica's plan. Now that something of a future had been secured for the group, that same spirit in Jago that willed him to stand up to the guard on the train car, had made him far more cavalier: he too was in the mood for revenge. But what revenge could be sought from machines, he thought. The city's power was in the minds of its subjects. Only a thin veil needed to be pulled down to free them. What a demonstration this could be, to liberate some of them. This would hurt the city most of all.

'I'm going to come with you,' Jago declared.

He sensed Amica stiffen.

'Why?' she said with poignancy.

Jago paused to consider his response.

Amica had told him once that the two of them had been thrown together by more than just fate. She had said they both possessed a drive, a leaning to anarchy that would forever push them towards each other. He had risked everything when he stood up against that guard; the embodiment of his oppression and his fears. And Amica, even after years as part of the machine, could not be manipulated beyond reprisal. She gave up all her privileges for him. They'd both held on to the vestiges of a life before the city and they strived for something that might resemble it again some day. But when Jago had actually found this, on the farm and now, at the village, he had never felt deserving of it: he felt like a cheat. In his journey to this new life, he had been mostly a passenger, particularly early on, and so he would always feel indebted to Amica for what she had done for him. It was a debt he could never repay. But if he could help her now, if he could lend himself to her for this, then at least that might be something.

'Amica,' he said, 'Did I tell you how hard it was for me to even reply to your first message? All that time ago? ...You know, I was so scared of what might happen. But...I did it anyway.'

Amica turned to face him.

'I used to pick the easy road,' he continued, 'I pretended everything was fine even when it wasn't. Then, when I met you, I chose to take the most difficult road, the most risky, with you. I could take that easy road again, and it would be even easier now with all we have here, but what kind of person would I be if I did that.'

The church muted again for a moment.

'Are you sure you want to come?' Amica asked.

Jago took Amica's hand in his and leaned towards her.

'I think I understand now,' he said, 'We can't just stop trying because *we're* okay, or *we've* got what we wanted. You risked everything for me, now I should do the same for someone else. If I were to turn my back on those still in the city, then I may as well turn my back on you.'

Amica put her other hand on his cheek, running her fingers down it.

'Sometimes we have to take a risk,' she whispered to him, 'We can't just live in fear forever. And when we do, that's when we find out who we are.'

She kissed him on the cheek, then their heads came together. Both of them closed their eyes.

Jago whispered back to her.

'I have everything I could ever want here, and everything I could ever need. But it doesn't mean that everything *else* is good, or everything *else* is right. If I'm no longer willing to stand up, then none of it means anything. You know you have nothing when there's nothing left you would fight for...and die for. And this is about something greater than us, this is about freedom.'

The vegetation had thatched thickly over the car. Otto and Amica had to clear a path through vines to reach it. Amica opened the driver seat door as far as she could until it was pinned in by branches. Otto reached over and braced it enough so that Amica could slip inside. He peaked through the window, seeing Amica retrieve a phone from the glove box. She turned it on.

'Just hope it's got some juice left,' she said.

The phone slowly booted up.

'How's Annia?' asked Amica, attempting to fill the wait.

'Why are you asking?' said Otto sharply.

'Oh, no reason.'

'Why? What do you know about her?'

'I don't know, what do you know?' She shook the phone, 'Ah, come on...,' she cursed.

'You know, don't you?' Otto queried wryly.

'Yes.' Amica looked up at him. 'Something to look forward to, I guess.'

'I guess.'

The phone lit up. Amica cycled through several screens then started to type.

'Won't they find out about this?" Otto asked.

'...*Four nights...,*' Amica mouthed the words she was typing, 'No they won't, we use a kind of cipher; code words.'

'Right. How many are we getting out?'

'Nine,' then she mouthed out loud again, '...*The usual. I like the park...*'

'And they'll come to meet you?'

'Yes..,' she gave him a glance, 'Well, hopefully.'

'Right.' Otto readjusted, the weight of the door pushing against him. 'So who's coming?'

'...*Favourite BBQ food?...*' she mouthed again. '...Hya, Jago, and Draven...'

'*Draven?* He really wants to join in on everything these days, doesn't he? And the dogs, coming along again?'

'I don't think we should take them, with what happened last time. We can't have them run off barking, especially as we'll be outside in the open.'

Amica showed the completed message to him, 'What do you think?'

Otto read from her phone, *'Four nights. The usual. I like the park. Favourite BBQ food?...'*

He looked at Amica, who looked pleased with herself.

'Well, it's certainly ambiguous,' he said.

'It means we'll meet in the park, there's one in our district,' explained Amica, 'That's where we used to meet up.'

'Okay, well, if they come, they come, I suppose,' Otto concluded, wanting to let go of the door now.

'Hope so,' Amica said under her breath, pressing the screen one last time, 'Sent,' she announced.

Then she looked up at Otto.

'There's no going back now,' she said, looking mutinous.

'Never,' he said.

7
PASSENGERS

1
THE RANGERS

He had nearly finished the seventh episode and had already guessed the ending. The archetypal anti hero; rugged, ribald, but loveable, would be killed off. And so he was, and in exactly the way Paine had predicted. The credits rolled and he got up from the sofa, shaking his head in disapproval. He went to the kitchen and took some popcorn from his cupboard — it was one of his privileges. Even over his tussling with the bag, he could hear the city messages during the intermission; they always seemed much louder than the programmes themselves. He looked over at the large lambent screen in the corner of his room. He'd seen this one before. There was fighting, fire and conflagration, which repeated, then a voice-over, which spoke in stentorian, motivating tones.

> 'STAY SAFE. STAY INSIDE.
> WE'RE STILL FIGHTING FOR YOU.
> ONLY TOGETHER WE CAN SAVE OUR CITY.'

The messages ended and episode eight began. Paine collapsed back onto the sofa, popcorn in hand. He watched, but his interest waned with the absence of the ill-fated major character, and his favourite. There was no tension any more, he felt, no antagonism between the main players. The show just plodded with prosiness.

Episode eight finished. Paine didn't move. More messages played.

This time, there were images of hospital wards, doctors and nurses sweating and looking harried, and many patients in beds. They were injured, bloodied or sick, and they stared meekly into the camera. The voice-over was piteous and pleading this time.

> 'CAN YOU LOOK THEM IN THE EYES?
> AND TELL THEM YOU DID EVERYTHING YOU COULD?

ONE DAY, THIS COULD BE SOMEONE *YOU* LOVE.
STAY SAFE. STAY INSIDE.'

Paine's phone vibrated on the floor next to him, stealing his attention. From his lain position he reached down to it, swiping over the screen. He frowned, then sat up straight, the last of his popcorn spilling over him. He re-read the message. It was from Amica.

Four nights.

The usual.

I like the park.

Favourite BBQ food?

This was the first time she had contacted him in over two years.

He had sometimes wondered about her, and had presumed the worst. He recalled their meeting years ago: she had opened her building door as he'd arrived delivering their food. They spoke, briefly and cautiously. But this would be the advent of a regular interaction between them. After she had gained enough of his confidence, he confessed to her that he had been speaking to several others too. His vocation allowed it: Paine was a supply driver for the district. Most were too frightened to speak to him when he buzzed their doors. But some weren't. And soon he'd formed a small network with him as its go between. The group started to communicate online, using an argot to mislead the algorithms — their locational commonality in conjunction with the keywords they might otherwise use would be vulnerable to flagging.

After some time, Paine decided that all of his befriended should actually meet; in person! Their local defunct park would provide the perfect cover, particularly the barbecue zone there, which was surrounded by trees and far enough away from the streets that the torches of the guards wouldn't see them. So they used the codeword *BBQ* in their messages to call a meeting. Only four attended on its maiden outing, and two of them were him and Amica. But by next time, there were six, then seven, then ten were regularly attending. All they did was talk to each other, occasionally shake hands or hug, but this alone was enough to provide them lasting felicity and leave them hungry for more. After several of these meet ups, the group started calling themselves, the park rangers. This was then shortened to just, the rangers.

But then, Amica seemed to drop out. She was not seen or heard from again, either at the park or at Paine's supply run to her building. He had messaged her, and so had many of the others, but there was never any response. Now, some two years later, she had finally messaged, and she'd even called for a meeting.

Paine was floored and unsure how to move forward. He wondered if it *was* really Amica first of all. He knew even just responding to her might put him and the others in danger. But if she *had* remained uncompromised all this time, then whatever her plans, he and the others would want to be party to it.

Episode nine was already about to finish, Paine had been deep in thought for its entire duration. He watched for a little longer but couldn't focus on it any more. It was just faces and mouths moving and contemplative stares, nothing but moving images housed in a rectangular border. There was no distinguishing between the TV and the wallpaper behind it, they were now just as uninteresting as the other.

The episode finally ended and the city messages played again.

This time, there were happy faces; all smiling and laughing. They were on their phones and behind their laptops, and they were chatting to each other online. Some were even dancing, some were singing, and they were all having a great time. Over the top was another voice; upbeat, saccharin and unctuous.

'THANK YOU TO ALL OUR STAY-INSIDE HEROES.
STAY SAFE AND BE HAPPY.
TOGETHER WE CAN.'

Paine picked up his phone and typed out a message for the rest of the rangers.

2
WAITING IN THE PARK

Paine left his room. He checked the lobby from the landing above, he couldn't see anyone coming. He went down the stairs, putting his weight on the bannisters so his steps wouldn't be heard on the old wood. He continued through the lobby to the entrance, also knowing where to tread to avoid the creaking floorboards. He peaked through a hole in the doorway, one he'd already burrowed through the boarding over the embrasure; there were no patrol lights outside.

He left the building and moved quickly across the street to the park. He saw the large sign over the entrance: HELP PROTECT OTHERS. DO NOT ENTER, then vaulted over the barrier and walked swiftly to the barbecue area. Ahead of him, a few feint shapes emerged in the soft light of the gloaming. They were fidgeting in the crisp autumn air.

'Paine, you made it,' Maia whispered to him as he went up to the three of them.

'Yes,' he responded, embracing her.

'What's going on then, Paine?' Cage asked him, as they shook hands.

'I don't know, she just messaged out of the blue,' Paine responded, 'said to meet tonight.'

'She's still stirring the pot then, looks like,' said Renata, as they shook hands also.

'Seems so.'

'I thought she was dead?' Cage added frankly.

Paine paused for a moment. 'Well, she still might be,' he thought aloud.

'Huh?' Caged then considered for a moment, 'So you think it might be some kind of set up then do you, Paine?'

Paine shrugged.

'Yet you're still here...?' noted Renata.

He shrugged again.

More arrived and soon a small crowd had formed in close propinquity. They each came up to Paine and the others, acknowledging them with a nod or a hand shake, then migrated away into their own groups. There was occasional hushed chatter amongst them but they stood mostly in silent anticipation. Paine looked over them. The moonlight barely highlighted them. They assumed ghostly figures in the darkness.

Maia then leaned in close to him, whispering again, 'I don't recognise quite a few of these people, there must be...sixty people turned up.'

'I think he's been busy recruiting again, Maia,' Cage chimed in.

'I didn't think so many would come,' admitted Paine, 'No one even knows what's going on.'

'It's better than doing nothing,' Maia defended him to Cage.

The four of them stood, filled with nervous excitement and anxiousness, amongst everyone gathered. They hadn't waited long when a buzz of activity spread from the edges of the crowd to them. Paine could hear his own name being hissed, and coming rushing towards him, snaking from person to person. It finally reached Cage standing beside him.

'Paine,' Cage said, 'she's here,' and he pointed to a tree in the distance.

Paine looked at each of them in turn.

'Okay, whatever happens,' he said, 'Good luck.'

He left them and weaved through the small crowd towards the tree. He could sense an air of uncertainty in the others but he couldn't give them any assurance, he had no idea what was going to happen either.

He emerged from the crowd and saw Amica and four others under the tree.

'Paine? What happened? There were only ten of us when I left,' Amica said in a loud whisper.

'Well, we've grown a bit,' he responded, 'you *have* been gone for two years.'

'Well, well done, I suppose,' she said. She gestured at the others, 'This is Jago, Otto, Hya, Draven.' Some nodded at him, some didn't. 'Everyone, this is Paine.'

Paine nodded back, then said, 'So, what's going on, Amica? We can't just stand here all night.'

'We're getting you all out of here,' she declared.

'Out of where?'

'Out of the city.'

'*Out of the city*?' How?' Paine said, eager.

'The subway, it's empty,' she explained, 'We're going under the city.'

'*Under the*—'

They heard shouting coming from the park entrance. They looked over as a wave of heads turned with them.

'What's going on here?' came a stout, peremptory voice from behind the barrier. It was so loud, even the farthest away of the rangers could hear it.

Two torches flashed through the crowd, then two guards vaulted the barrier and marched towards them.

'Back inside, all of you!' one of them shouted, 'You'll all be corrected for this!'

Paine watched as the crowd backed away, but then pause, realising their vast numbers. The front row seemed to straighten up defiantly. Then they paced towards the guards. The next row followed, then the next. The guards backed away, took one look at each other, then turned and fled.

Paine looked back to Amica. She was tapping the side of her thigh nervously.

'What have they done?' she said.

'What?' one of the others questioned.

'They'll just come back, with reinforcements,' Amica portended, 'They've seen our numbers now, they'll double them, at least.'

The five of them shared wary glances.

'We can't use the subway any more,' she added, 'They'll just follow us down there, we'll have nowhere to go.'

Then came a new voice.

'I think I know how we can lose them.'

'Draven?' Amica said after a moment.

A chortled laugh came from someone else, 'You've barely said a word for two years and now you speak up...?' he said.

'Otto!' the one next to him reprimanded.

'We can get the train,' said Draven, 'go to the outskirts. We can lose them. I know how to operate them. Trust me.'

'A *train*?' Otto rolled his eyes.

'Yes, it's nearly morning, it will be at the platform.'

Otto shook his head, looked at Amica, 'Is he serious?'

Amica considered the idea, tapping her thigh with even more rapidity.

'He's right,' said the only one who hadn't spoken, 'We know the station, we know we can get to the outskirts, I've done it many times. We can make it to the river from there.'

'Fine,' Amica decided after the shortest of pauses, 'let's do it! I don't know what other choice we have.' Then she addressed Paine, 'Tell them we have to go to the train station.'

Paine spun away from them. With no time to think about it, he cupped his hands around his mouth. 'Train station!' he shouted - he wasn't worried about making noise now - 'Go to the train station!'

Others echoed the instruction and it permeated the park.

'We need to hurry,' warned Amica, 'they'll be coming soon.'

3
BOARDING THE TRAIN

They overcrowded the station entrance, banged on the shutters and tore them asunder. Then they smashed the glass panels and flooded into the main terminal. Once they were inside, Jago and Amica were hastened to the front to lead them and so the crowd arrived at the security gate to the platform. The light was red, but it didn't matter this time; the masses clawed the boards away and kicked through the barrier. They squeezed through the gaps they'd made and ran to the waiting train. But the carriage doors were sealed. They tried, but they could not prise them open.

'Draven, where's Draven?' Jago shouted and Draven emerged from the crowd 'What do we do?' he asked him.

'Follow,' he instructed and the two of them eddied a path back to an area just beside the platform entrance. There was a control panel at the base of one of the support towers and Draven started to operate it. Jago glanced back at the others as they tried helplessly to board the train, then back at Draven. He felt powerless and was clueless to what Draven was doing.

'Look out! Safeties!' a voice shouted.

Through the broken panels in the barrier, Jago saw a mass of guards storming into the station, numbering perhaps over a hundred. The guards chased down and floored those still in the terminal, pinning them to the ground. Others tried to free them, but were quickly overwhelmed too. The batons struck out wildly at whatever they could. Many of the rangers were dragged behind a wall of uniforms.

The guards marched on towards the platform.

Jago spun back to Draven. He was desperate but didn't want to rush him into a mistake. He looked at the train, the boards over the windows had been broken but the glass remained unyielding. Then he turned back to the security gate; some of the rangers had gone back to brace it, trying to slow the coming guards.

'Pull here when I say,' came Draven's still steady voice.

Jago turned to him and gripped the lever as he was told.

'Now, pull,' said Draven.

Jago did so.

Draven danced his hands over the console, ending with a flourish.

'That should do it,' he said.

There was a rumbling. It filled the hanger. It was felt in the ground and for just a moment, seemed to stop everyone in their tracks, even the guards. The train shuddered with life and started to glow. Then in unison, all the train doors parted. Light streamed out onto the platform.

'Get them all on!' Draven shouted, 'I'll get it going,' and he shooed Jago away.

Jago nodded, then rushed towards Amica on the platform.

'Get everyone on,' he shouted to her, still a distance away, 'it's going.'

He saw Amica acknowledge, then direct Hya, Paine and Otto next to her to different carriages. They moved to their places and started to help the others board.

Bodies poured onto the train.

The guards were beginning to punch through the blockade at the barrier and debouch out onto the platform. They overwhelmed the ones left trying to stop them, yanking them down or throwing them back into the sea of guards behind.

'They're through!' Amica shouted back at Jago, who was still half way between her and Draven.

Jago turned once more to Draven. They needed to go. Now!

'Draven!' he heckled.

Draven was still absorbed in the controls but raised a thumbs up to Jago.

The train spluttered into motion and started to move off.

'Hurry, get them on!' Draven shouted at him, 'And you too. Go!'

Jago turned and ran the rest of the way to Amica.

The remaining rangers sprinted for the open carriage doors as the train began to leave the platform. The guards chased them.

Jago caught up to Amica and they ran to Otto.

'We need to stop the guards from boarding,' Jago shouted at him, 'I'll go—!'

But before Jago could finish, Otto pushed both of them onto the train. The ones already on board then pulled them into the safety of the carriage.

'We'll sort it,' Otto insisted, 'Just look after the others.'

The carriage moved away from the platform before Amica and Jago could argue with him.

Otto then looked to the far end of the platform and saw Paine. He urgently waved him on too and Paine obeyed, jumping onboard.

Otto turned back to the security barrier and saw the melee between the guards and the rangers. Amidst it, he saw Hya, as she dragged a ranger back and shoved him towards the carriage doors.

Otto couldn't get her attention. He ran over to her and grabbed her arm. She turned.

'We gotta go!' he shouted at her.

The guards were nearly on them. Some were jumping onto the last carriage as it moved away behind them.

'Now!' Otto yelled.

'Wait,' Hya said, pointing, 'Draven's still there.'

Otto looked and saw Draven still by the control panel.

'There's no time!' he shouted at her again.

He pulled on Hya's arm but she pulled it free.

The guards descended on Draven in the distance.

'What's he doing? Draven?' she called.

There was no response.

A guard struck Draven on the shoulder and he fell to a knee. He pivoted and was able to push the guard away. He went back to the panel, operating it again. Then two more guards came beside him, grabbing him around both arms. They yanked him back and threw him along the ground.

'Draven!' Hya screamed. She went to run to him, but found she couldn't.

Otto had grabbed her around the waist and lifted her up, she had no purchase to go forward. Otto shifted a few steps behind him, Hya still in his arms. Then he fell back, judging the passing train door behind them.

They collapsed into the carriage together.

The train gained speed and pulled away from the station. The remaining guards were left collected at the platform's edge, watching as the train fled.

Hya pulled herself free from her and Otto's entanglement and got up.

'Draven, we have to go back for him!' she cried at him.

'Watch out!' shouted Otto, seeing behind her.

Hya turned. A guard barged her towards the still open doorway, trying to push her off the moving train! She managed to divert them into the door frame instead and they slammed into the side of the carriage. Hya felt her back crunch against it. Otto then came up behind them, grabbed any two folds he could find in the guard's uniform, and threw it off the train.

Hya had fallen to a knee, her back giving out. Otto lifted her up onto one of the seats. They both looked back down the carriage to see more rangers fighting the guards that had boarded. They tussled but the guards were too many. The others were beaten down and discarded out onto the tracks.

The guards then came at Hya and Otto. Otto eyed the opposite end of the carriage where there was refuge. Another group were standing there, readying themselves to charge at the guards.

'Don't, stop!' Otto shouted at them, seeing their attack would be futile, 'Keep going. Into the next carriage!' He waved them back towards the internal door.

They heeded his call and went to it, but the door was unresponsive. They managed to just force it open enough so the first of them could get through.

The guards were nearly on Otto and Hya. Otto picked up Hya on his shoulder and ran over to the others. He fell and Hya tumbled out in front of him. Turning, he saw a guard had caught his leg and pulled him down. He was being dragged away from Hya. He kicked out and the guard was repelled. Then he rolled onto his front, looked up and shouted to the others again.

'Take her through,' he commanded, '*Her*! She's wounded!'

Another guard stood over Otto and struck down onto his back with its baton. Otto winced in pain. He turned onto his back, tripping the guard down as he did. The baton spilled out of its hand as they struggled. The guard mounted him and reined down punches as Otto tried to guard. He could feel the metal ridges of its gloves dig into his arms and his ribs. His defence weakened as the back of his head was pummelled into the floor of the train.

He just managed to slide his position underneath and push the guard back over him. He came to his knee, expecting to fight it, but the guard had kept moving forward and was now bearing down on the others...and Hya! They saw it coming and tried to hurry, but they had to go one by one as they squeezed through the small opening they'd made.

Otto ran for the guard and jumped on its back and they fell forward to the floor. He put his arm under its chin to subdue it. He looked up again.

'Her! Get her through!' he barked at the others.

They scrambled and at his behest, prioritised Hya. They pushed her through the opening and outside onto the thin platform between the two carriages. The others ahead of her had begun to prise open the door to the next carriage and were starting to board it. Hya tried desperately to pull herself back seeing that Otto was in trouble, but her back wouldn't let her; she could barely move.

The guard below Otto wriggled around trying to free itself. Otto pressed down and grounded its head into the floor. Then he felt another blow to his back, a second guard had come up behind him. The pain shot through him, but he stayed clutched to the one underneath. A third guard then came passed them, heading towards the end of the carriage again. Otto rolled into its path to stop it, managing to knock it into the row of seats.

The standing guard swung for him. He tried to move but was still entangled with the other two. The baton struck him on the arm. Then again on the shoulder. And then again, and again. He tried to lift himself free from the mass of bodies.

Then he lost all feeling.

His ears rung and he saw blood.

He looked up. He couldn't see Hya any more.

He was dazed but could make out the blurred outline of another guard in the now dimmed light, it had nearly reached the doorway! Otto winced and with whatever strength he had left, he lashed at the shapes around him, freeing himself. He stumbled forward, then dived at the guard ahead, grabbing its leg, and felling it. He climbed over but it turned, got on top of him and held him face down to the floor.

Otto dragged himself forward, the guard still on his back, and managed to reach the end of the carriage. He pulled his head and shoulders through the opening and over the precipice. He could see the flashing tracks running below him. Then he felt a foot stomp down onto his back.

He couldn't move.

He looked up to see the others now all in the next carriage. They reached for him over the threshold. But he was too far away.

Otto felt another blow and the shooting pain again. He was just able to free his arms over the lip of the opening. He was searching for something below. Then he found it and grabbed it with both hands.

He glanced up again and saw Hya in the crowd with the others; she was still trying to get to him. Then she froze suddenly, realising what he was about to do.

Otto winked at Hya, wanting her to remember that.

Then he pulled the lever below him.

The carriages separated.

Otto's carriage kept pace for a few moments but then began to lag behind.

Hya went blank. The others let go of her, knowing she couldn't get back to him now. She collapsed to her knees and watched on.

Otto was still on the floor with the swarm of guards around him, their uniforms filled the carriage. With one last effort, he rotated his body under the guard's foot and got up. He elbowed one guard closest to him. Another one struck him down. He got up again. He kept fighting, hitting out at whatever moved.

The carriage drifted away, further and further from Hya, and slowly darkening. Still, she saw the embattled Otto; but smaller and smaller, and harder and harder for her to see. There was nothing she could do.

Then finally, Hya couldn't see him at all any more. She couldn't see the carriage and couldn't hear any more sounds of fighting. Only the darkness of the tunnel remained and the sound of the tracks below.

4
RETURN JOURNEY

Amica and Jago hurried back through the carriages, panicked guards may still be aboard. Each door slowed them down as they prised it open. They squeezed through one more door then stopped unexpectedly. What they thought was the penultimate carriage was not, they were at the trains' end. They could hear the raucous gale from the outside and a bruised doorway flailed from the opening ahead of them. A figure was knelt in front of it, it looked out into the tunnel's dark abyss. They filed through a small group that had congregated and saw that the figure was Hya.

'Hya? What happened?' Amica said as she crouched beside her.

She put a hand on Hya's shoulder but Hya flinched it away and turned sharply from her. Amica retreated, got back to her feet, feeling shunned. She looked around at the others and saw someone she knew.

'Ledger? What happened here?' she said.

'I'm not sure,' Ledger replied, 'This guy...he fought them off, then separated the carriages. He took them with him. They'd have taken the train otherwise, for sure.'

'Who?' she asked, though she was almost certain who it was, 'Who's *this guy*?'

'Don't know,' Ledger replied, 'He wasn't one of us.'

Amica looked at Jago, then they heard another voice.

'Otto,' it said, 'his name was Otto.'

Hya slowly rose to her feet, cutting a warped figure. Her body was twisted to one side and one shoulder drooped below the other. She moved uncouthly towards Ledger, one leg dragging as she walked. Her eyes were fixed on him.

'Otto,' she said again, with bile in her tongue, 'His name was Otto. And no, he wasn't *one of you*,' she shifted her eyes over to Amica, 'He was one of us.'

'Hya,' Amica said, her heart aching for her. She couldn't help but move to comfort her, but at once Hya raised her hands and pushed her away. Amica fell back onto the seats.

'This is your fault,' Hya crowed at her, 'I don't know any of these people. They're *your* people. Not mine.' She looked around the group. '*Amica has to save her friends*,' she said in a scathing, mocking accent, 'Well, you couldn't save Otto, could you? And you couldn't save Draven either.'

'Draven?' Amica mouthed in shock.

'Yes, Draven. You didn't even know, did you? You don't even notice. Well, he's probably dead too. They both sacrificed themselves, for all *your* people.'

Amica found herself in turmoil. She couldn't master the emotions that were pervading her: the pain she herself felt at the loss, her sympathy for Hya and her guilt for what had happened.

She didn't know what to do, anything she said would only anger Hya further, but she was desperate to appease her. She just stood, stranded, looking back at her.

Hya shook her head in disgust and turned her back. She dragged herself away through the crowd, limping as she went through to the next carriage. No one went to help her.

Jago and Amica looked at each other.

'Draven? Otto?' said Amica, overcome.

Jago had decided this couldn't be the time to think about them. He looked back at Amica temperately.

'We need to check where we're going,' he said coldly, 'Paine was near the front. Ledger,' - he'd remembered his name - 'Did you see him board?'

'Yes, he made it on, at the front like you said,' he answered.

'Okay, we're going through,' Jago said, turning to Amica.

She was staring out to the tunnel, the occasional light projecting over her face.

'Amica?' Jago repeated.

There was no response. She had disengaged.

'...Does it say where we're going?' Paine asked the others.

Maia, Gage, Renata and he were all in the driver compartment of the train. They could see through the window onto the tracks, the immediate area ahead lit up by the train lights.

'Yes, there's a map here,' Maia answered, 'on this screen, we're going to the outskirts. That sounds right, right?'

Cage raised his eyebrows, 'Could be. We haven't seen any of Amica's lot yet. They were the ones with the plan.'

'Yes, I'm sure one of them said *the outskirts*,' said Paine, 'Would make sense if we're leaving the city.'

The door slid open. It was Jago. He recognised Paine.

'Everyone okay?' he said.

They nodded.

'We're going to the outskirts, right?' Maia asked him.

'Yes, it should be on this line,' Jago confirmed, 'Is that what it says?'

'Yes. And you said we go to a *river or something after that*?'

'Yes, there's a farm there. It will have some supplies we left behind. We can rest there for a bit, then head onto the village.'

'*Village*?' enquired Cage.

'Yes, we live there.'

'You think we'll get any trouble at the outskirts?' added Paine.

'No, there's usually no safeties there, they don't bother patrolling it.'

Jago looked at the screen. There was a green light flashing and a blue circle just away from it. The green light was moving very rapidly towards the blue circle.

The others were watching him.

'It's Jago, right...?' said Maia. He nodded. 'So..., does anyone in your group know how to stop a train?'

The green light kept moving.

'No,' replied Jago, 'not any more.'

A wall of light hit the train. It was now daytime and the tunnel was suddenly far behind them. The battered and splintered boards hung down below the carriage windows, clattering against the sides of the train as it moved. Its passengers were now blessed with an unobscured gallery of the outdoors through the openings. But they went with no less rapidity. Buildings flashed passed them. The passengers waited in suspense. Then fewer and fewer buildings passed. They were nearly at the outskirts station.

Then, a mechanical grinding sound came from somewhere underneath them. It was noisy and felt heavy under their feet. The train was braking. It began to slow.

Jago lurched forward, just stopping short of crashing into the front window. He steadied himself and watched as the station came into view. He crossed himself, reserving a special prayer for Draven, who must have programmed the train to stop here.

They arrived into the outskirts, the lights in the carriages coming up again. The survivors debarked through the still open doorways and passed through the terminal.

Jago stepped out from the security entrance, half expecting a car to be waiting for him. He looked out over the surroundings. They were the same as always: a decimated mess; a ruin. He had always felt daunted by them, standing amidst the urban relics and the unorganised damage. But now, he didn't feel anything, it was all merely circumstantial.

Amica led them; now a band of maybe forty, from the outskirts and out of the city. Though Amica had once told the others that the perimeter was apocryphal — which had then spread to the rest of the rangers — it hadn't stopped some of them walking in perpetual dread of it.

A horizon of barren dirt appeared ahead of them and as they walked, even in late autumn, their dry beseeching mouths thirsted for water. Amica had only brought enough supplies for ten, not for four times that! Their earlier efforts had also taken their toll and the group were quickly tiring. Amica saw no option but to now reach the river as soon as they could; she could treat the water there and the group could drink and cool down. She abandoned her caution and upped the pace to a nearly intolerably degree.

Gratefully, the sweetness of the countryside soon cosseted them, and this instantly steeled the spirit of the group. Then at last, the river, like a beacon, sparkled into view as the sunlight twinkled over it.

They had forgotten all about the perimeter.

Hya had seen it all before. She stood back from the water and far away from the others. She couldn't bear to be near them, and certainly not share in their ecstasy. She'd watched the familiar sight of them make for the water; bounding and falling in. Then they disported: splashed around, swam, lazed and carried on in front of her. Every joy that they took from their pyrrhic victory hurt her and flaunted their ignorance of *her* loss. The more they pranced, the more she hated them. If she could undo it all, this entire escapade, to have Otto and Draven back, she would. She begged the river to sweep and wash the rangers away, if it could only bring her back her friends.

She thought also of Annia, and Bodhi, and the agony that awaited them. She had seen resignation before; she had seen it in Jonet's eyes when she'd told her the death of her husband. Jonet had been broken by a grief too heavy to comprehend and too deep to reconcile. Could Bodhi and Annia endure what was coming for them? And could she stand to see their suffering?

Amica hadn't attempted to speak to Hya since they'd disembarked, she knew there was no consoling her. She could only wait patiently and hope for the rift to seal in time. Hya's onslaught had continued to gnaw at her, she felt exposed by it. She *had* been selfish, she *had* risked the writers for her own ends. She'd always thought of the rescue as nothing but altruistic, but not any more. She hadn't considered this was *her* story, Jago, Otto, Draven and Hya, and even the others, they were all just playing a bit part in it.

Amica had been quiet during the journey and hadn't spoken a word to anybody. Like Hya, she had stayed back from the water and away from the others. Watching them, she should have felt endlessly proud of her eclat; she had saved them, they were liberated because of her. But inside, was only a twisting guilt as she thought of Otto and Draven, and Annia and Bodhi, and Annia's child. She thought of their approaching sorrow, and she thought of Hya's scorn.

5
COMING HOME

Paine was behind Maia, Cage and Renata as they walked. The river was behind them, and so was the farm. Paine looked ahead through the woods, the tree tops were framing a distant church spire. The village was close.

They kept on and finally came out from the woods. The church and its auspices were now in full view. The morning light reflecting brightly in the church window bestilled Paine and he stopped and gazed at the numinous structure in front of him. He then closed his eyes and embraced the sensation that had come over him. He could hear the sound of trickling water, the rustling of plants, and birds in conversation. He hadn't noticed them until now.

'Pretty amazing, isn't it?' commented Maia, who had come back for him, noticing he had stopped.

'Can you hear that?' said Paine, 'The birds, they seem so loud...'

Maia smiled and said, 'That's because we've never really listened before.'

Cage and Renata also came back to join them.

'You two okay?' Cage asked.

'Yes, fine,' said Maia.

Cage looked around at the buildings, adding irreverently, 'Wonder if we'll get a house each.'

'Unlikely, Cage,' said Renata.

A door creaked open from the house nearest them, a head peaked out from inside it. It looked over the lines of people that were approaching the church, then looked back, inadvertently meeting eyes with Paine.

Paine felt he should say something.

'Hi,' he said, as pleasantly as he could.

'Hi,' the head responded cautiously.

Two more heads then appeared below the other, about two-thirds the way down the doorway.

'Look at all the people,' one of them said, open mouthed.

'Mummy,' the other one said, 'are we being invaded?' it asked in all earnestness.

'Um,' the higher up head said, 'I don't know, Freya, why don't you ask the nice man...?'

Paine tried to smile at them but he was unpracticed, and in his best diffusing voice he said, 'No, we're not invading, we're friends of Amica.'

'She said there would only be nine of you,' the mother questioned accusingly.

Paine wasn't sure how to answer.

'This man recruited us,' Maia spoke up, 'After Amica left, we grew in numbers. Amica is at the church now, she can explain. Trust me, we hate the city just as much as you do.'

'Okay...well...that's fine then, I suppose,' the higher up head concluded. There was an awkward pause. 'Well, we'll probably see you later then. Bye.'

'Yes, bye,' Maia added as the door began to shut.

The lower heads waved enthusiastically at them, 'Bye,' they chorused.

They were promptly shepherded inside and the door creaked closed on them.

Paine, Maia, Renata and Cage were propelled by the others through the small audience that had gathered in the village square. They had embayed Amica and Jago who were in discussion, as they waited for some kind of announcement.

The six of them stood at the front of the crowd.

'This one might be a bit hard to explain to the others,' Amica said to Jago.

'Well, we'll have to just tell them as we see them,' Jago responded, 'I'm sure they've already seen them anyway.'

'What do you need us to do?' Paine contributed.

Amica turned to him.

'Did you see Hya somewhere?' she asked.

'No, 'fraid not.'

'Okay, well, you can help them find somewhere to stay,' Amica said, 'even if it's just to sleep tonight, we can sort it all tomorrow. They can live in groups, alone, whatever they want. We have plenty of space. The main thing is that everyone has a roof over their heads.'

'Okay.'

Paine went to leave but then hesitated. He scanned around everyone gathered.

'How many of us made it?' he asked Amica sombrely.

'Maybe forty,' she estimated.

Paine looked around at the rangers again. They looked back at him and he felt an expectation on him to say something. He thought about it then assumed a promontory figure in front of them. The responsibility of the occasion suddenly made him nervous. They were waiting for his summary.

'Well, we made it,' he began, hesitantly, 'We went a bit further than the park this time, right?' - a few laughs were heard - 'But let's not forget those that didn't make it, those that sacrificed themselves so that the rest of us could be here.'

There was an impromptu moment of silence.

'We need to sort out accommodation,' he continued, 'So decide who you want to live with…or, live on your own, there are plenty of houses. We'll help you.'

He paused, then added, 'And…and…explore the area…explore the fields, the woods, the river, roam as you please and as far as you wish. No more rules, no more lockdown, we are free now.'

Shortly after, the crowd was humming with chatter and pontification as they decided where to live and who to live with. Then behind them, the door of the cottage by the rectory opened and Ever and Cleo walked out. The ones nearest to them turned and looked at them and their eyes widened in disbelief. Then the ones next to them turned too and froze. Soon the focus of the whole crowd was on Cleo and Ever and silence descended. For in Cleo's arms, was baby Jett.

The three of them processed slowly towards the church. The people parted in awe.

Cleo and Ever were shy from the attention but smiled courteously. They understood the reaction, having been the same when they first saw Cato.

They went to Amica and Jago and shuffled behind them to be less conspicuous.

With Ever and Cleo lending their hand also, the rangers were all re-homed. Most slept almost immediately once they'd passed the threshold of their new accommodation. They were depleted and in need of repose. A few however, infused with the elixir of curiosity and intrigued by the exoticism of their new world, went off exploring. Some, fascinated to know the native villagers, went to the square and talked with the writers and Amica and Jago. They all seemed so foreign to the new arrivals, in manner and temperament. They were so confident, and embracing of them, something they hadn't experienced for a very long time. The three dogs would also make an appearance in the square. When word spread they were there, many of the rangers came back out from their housing to witness them. They were amazed at what they were seeing.

But by night time, all had returned inside for that haven of rest, which welcomes the weary laden and the well travelled. The village was serene again, its sudden influx now unnoticeable. Its paths and avenues empty and only the tireless work of the stream over the stones marred the perfect quiet.

Paine, who had awoken from a short slumber, went outside from the house he was sharing with Maia, Renata and Cage. He breathed in the night and the clean air and observed the grey tincture of the moon light. Then he saw two figures sitting on the benches in the square a short distance away. One was Amica, who had her hand on the back of the other, consoling her. The other he did not recognise. She had her head in her hands and drew a lacrymose figure. Paine wondered who she was.

Maia had woken too and came outside to join him. She then saw what he saw, as the two on the bench were now embracing each other.

'Who do you think she is?' she whispered to Paine, though she already had an idea.

She put her hand on his shoulder and he put his hand on her hand.

'Someone who knew Otto pretty well, I'm guessing,' Paine responded. Then they both noticed her abdomen. 'And I'm thinking that he was the father of that child too.'

Paine looked down as he realised, needing to look away from the pitiful scene. Maia put her arm around his waist and Paine, his arm around her shoulder, and they came together. Paine kissed her on the forehead as she rested her head on his shoulder. They stood for a while contemplating how life was prone to such cruel circumstance.

Earlier that day, Rumer had been looking after Cato and Djuna when she saw the many new faces appear in the village. Her fears were eased when she saw Amica and Jago with them. She wanted to find out who they were but couldn't leave the children until she was relieved from her baby sitting.

As she watched from her window, the door to the house suddenly flew open, nearly cracking into the wall. Hya had barged in. She said nothing and passed hurriedly through to the other room. Rumer knew instantly she was beyond petty irritation and she followed to check on her.

'Hya, what happened?' she said.

'Otto...Draven...gone.'

'What? Who's gone?'

'And now we've got this lot,' huffed Hya, ignoring the question.

'You mean the people in the square? Who *are* they exactly?'

'Amica's friends, I don't know. There were only supposed to be nine, now there's about fifty!'

Rumer couldn't understand her. She tried again.

'Fifty what? Hya, what happened back there?'

'It was supposed to be easy: go underground, come back, that's it. Then the safeties showed up, we had to escape, so we took the train.'

'*The train*?' Rumer was lost.

'Yes, Draven suggested it, he could get them out on the train, he said. Well, stupid idea that was, now he's probably dead.'

Hya then seemed to spasm and she crumpled to a knee. Rumer went to her—

'No, I'm fine, I'm fine,' Hya seethed.

Rumer persisted, 'What do you mean? What happened to Draven? Hya, what's wrong with you, you can barely stand.'

Hya sat down on the floor, pressing her back against the wall to try to alleviate the pain.

'I told you already,' she said, 'They're gone, Draven, Otto, gone! And I probably broke my back or something...'

'You broke your back?' exclaimed Rumer.

'One of the safeties attacked me, tried to throw me off the train! So Otto jumped in. Of course he did, the macho man he is. And now he's gone too, cos he's such a hero and all that, and I'm still here, and he's not. *I* was the one who broke my back. *I* was the one who was useless and couldn't move. And *I* made it? And he didn't. How does that work?'

Hya then prostrated herself, lying down on the floor, trying to stretch out.

'What a waste,' she said, softer this time, 'And all for these people we don't even know.'

'The new people, right... Have you spoken to any of them?'

'No, why would I?'

There was a knock at the door. Rumer left the room to get it. Hya tried to move but felt the pain again. She wasn't even convinced she could get up of her own accord now. She heard the door open, then Amica's voice. She couldn't allow Amica to see her like that. She forced herself up through the pain anyway.

She heard Jago's voice too, they had come to collect the children. Pleasantries were exchanged, then she heard Rumer give her away. She braced herself for another confrontation.

Amica entered the room.

'Hya,' she started...

'You don't need to say anything,' Hya spoke over her, 'I don't do these kind of conversations. We don't need to talk.'

Amica looked at Hya, wishing she could make everything okay again.

'Have you told Annia yet?' Hya asked her.

'No, no one's seen her,' Amica replied, 'I will talk to her later.'

They stood in silence for a moment, neither budging.

'Just go, okay,' Hya said at last, 'You got what you wanted, didn't you? Now take your kids and get out.'

Amica was wounded by Hya's obloquy, she desperately wanted to resolve this. But a crying Djuna tore her away and she begrudgingly left the room.

As soon as Amica could no longer see her, Hya collapsed back onto the floor, managing to seat herself up against the wall again. She overheard the goodbyes from the next room, then the door close again and the crying fade away. Rumer came rushing back into the room and got down beside her. She rested her head on Hya's lap and they sat still for a while.

'I'm sorry they're gone, Hya,' Rumer said delicately, then turned onto her back so she was looking up at Hya's face. 'You should get someone to take a look at your back.'

Hya was warmed by Rumer's comely concern and earnest affection. She looked back down at her.

'Thank you, Ru,' she said.

6
A VISITOR FROM THE CITY

After Amica had left her after their conversation, Annia stayed outside till nearly morning. Her and Otto had shared a home and she couldn't face it and be reminded of him. It was so late now that it was early, and the keenest of birds had started to sing. Her body was chilled to its core and shaking, she had to move inside. She was loathe to wake them, but she had no place else she wanted or felt she could go. Annia would burden Rumer and Hya with her untimely presence.

They took her in that morning with commiseration and such welcoming that she felt unworthy of it. Her and Hya shared a common grief for the loss of Otto and were bound in mutual empathy. She was adopted into their household and stayed with them as the days became weeks and the weeks became seasons.

Another winter passed and in the early spring, Annia gave birth to her and Otto's daughter. She named her Odette in honour of her father. Cleo and Ever soon followed suit in the summer, giving birth to their second child, a girl named Sage. Paine and Maia, who had been together since the early formation of the rangers, had a baby boy the next autumn, and called him Macon. Renata and Cage, who, having known each other from the rangers, coupled together and moved out of the shared house with Maia and Paine when Macon arrived — they moved into the house next door. A fecund Ever and Cleo again added to *their* brood, nearly three years after their second, naming the new boy, Kai.

Forty two people had made it to the village. No one was sure exactly how many people had congregated in the park that night, so the true devastation at the station could never fully be documented. Of the ones who had survived, and those of child bearing age, they too began to have children in the years that followed their relocation to the village. When this second generation grew up and became adults, they were handed the care of the village. And when *they* had children of *their* own, a third generation was welcomed.

Cato, the eldest child of Jago and Amica, coupled with Odette, the child of Otto and Annia. Through some notion of primogeniture, Cato inherited the run of the rectory when he became a young man and Amica and Jago moved into one of the smaller houses. He and Odette lived there happily for many years and soon, Jago and Amica would be given a grandchild, a boy named Levi; honourably chosen to continue the trend of vowel sound ending names in the family. Djuna, Jago and Amica's second child, coupled with Macon, Maia and Paine's only child. Djuna and Macon had two children; one called Mason, after his father, and another called Bena. Jett, the first born of Ever and Cleo, coupled with a second generation ranger, called Mariah. And to them was born a girl called Everleigh, named in honour of her grandfather. Ever and Cleo's second born, Sage, also coupled with a young ranger, Miller, and they had a girl called Taryn. And finally, their last born, Kai, partnered with Jamila, another ranger offspring. Two years after their first, Jett and Mariah had a second child, a boy named Logan, and then a third boy, in another two years, called Jaxon.

Annia had once asked unironically if the children would soon outnumber the adults. They did, and soon the population of the village had outgrown it. They built what extra accommodation they could but some of the villagers began to emigrate. They left in hopes of starting their own communities in other liveable dwellings outside the city. Amica had replied to Annia all those years ago, that that was very much the idea, that the children *would* outnumber them. Amica had always dreamed that the children would inherit the land that they had procured for them, and made fruitful, and that they would prosper on it and be enriched. Generations did prosper in the village and the noble stories of its past and its people were never forsaken.

Amica and Hya wouldn't speak for some time after their confrontation at the house. Though they would see each other in the village, Amica never broached the subject of their disharmony, knowing it would only push Hya further away.

The beginnings of their reconciliation came in the unlikely shape of Fox. His unique bond with Hya since they'd met in the subway made her more susceptible to his casuistry. With this, and a scheme appropriate of his age in brazen but not in cunning, he was able to orchestrate a first interaction between the two of them in almost a year.

He had insisted to both of them separately that, for his twelfth birthday, they must attend a celebration party on the field closest to the village. Amica had asked him why have it outside when it might rain. He said that it was *his* birthday, and not to ask questions.

So Amica and Hya turned up to Fox's birthday party to discover that they were the only ones there. They found themselves face to face, standing either side of a small table, with Fox as mediator. They couldn't help share the levity of this rather risible situation, not to mention the embarrassment at having been duped by a pre-adolescent.

Nothing had really changed though, Hya would never be interested in ironing out old barb and neither really was Amica now. They sat down at the table and no words were spoken. Fox served them drinks and perhaps just to humour him, they clinked their cups together and drank. Fox left them alone in stale silence.

Eventually it was broken by Amica.

She spoke uncontested for some time and she even wondered if her words were landing. She confessed to Hya that she was once a guard, and that Hya was now privy to a secret only her and Jago knew. This experience had shaped her, she explained, and she would always harbour some guilt for what she was. She explained how the rangers had inadvertently saved her. In embracing the charm of their basal connections and witnessing their grace under hardship, she realised the verisimilitude of her character: she realised she had become monstrous herself. She felt she owed the rangers, and though she tried, she couldn't just leave them behind and forget about them. She had to save them, as they had her.

Hya understood and really, she had always understood. What difference was there really between her and Amica? Had she not risked the lives of the writers many times over? Had they not risked *their* lives for her too? Talon, Ophelia and Caius had all likely died, even if indirectly, because of her. But would any of those three have had it any other way? Would they choose to still be prisoners? The dead are at least free.

Fox returned. Amica asked him where he had been and he replied that he'd been at his *real* birthday party, at his house, with all the other villagers. The two adults were amused by this and this further disarmed them.

Though they were very different, Hya and Amica were inextricably connected by what they had done. They might be from opposing sides, but they were of the same coin.

After this meeting, old wounds started to heal over time and they began to socialise in the same circles again. As Rumer cohabitated with Annia and her child, and given the numerousness with which Amica's children, Cato and Djuna, play-dated with Odette, continuing to evade Amica would have been a challenge for Hya anyway. So from a kinship of respect and admiration, evolved a lasting friendship between them.

Though distraught with the news of Otto's passing, it was Annia who searched out Bodhi first after the events at the train station and told him about Draven. Left with the news, Bodhi felt as if he was all alone again, just as he had been for most of his life. He had lived in a kind of exile since his friends and family were all taken to the city, tortured by solitary and endless time. Now, just as he had welcomed the embrace of company once again, those same crippling feelings of abandonment and loneliness had returned.

Annia continued to reach out to him but Bodhi stayed locked away. He wouldn't speak to anyone and fell into a deep depression. But, by some miraculous grace of good fortune, Bodhi would soon be saved from his shadows.

One day, Jago and Amica were walking through the woods just away from the village. They were hand in hand and the lushness of a radiant summer engrossed them. Appearing a distance ahead of them, was a figure they didn't recognise. They had never had any wanderers passing by before.

They were wary and stopped in their tracks.

The figure continued moving just ahead of them.

'Who are you?' shouted Jago.

The stranger jumped, then turned to them slowly.

'Me?' she said, 'I-who are *you*?'

She seemed flustered. Jago and Amica looked at each other.

'We live here,' Amica answered, 'Where have you come from?'

'You *live here*?' the stranger said surprised, 'I came from the city, I thought you did too...'

'*The city*? No,' said Jago.

'What do you mean, *you came from the city*?' Amica asked her.

'Well, I mean, I left the city,' she replied, 'Same as everyone.'

Amica and Jago couldn't make sense of her.

'*Everyone*?' questioned Jago.

'Yes, everyone.' She paused, then checked, 'So you live here?'

'Yes.'

'And you didn't come from the city?'

'Not recently, no,' answered Amica.

'And no one else has come this way?'

'No...'

'So that means...if you didn't come from the city, then...'

The stranger became visibly excited, her inhibitions seemed to be superseded by whatever she'd just realised.

'You don't know, do you?' she exclaimed, 'You don't know what happened?'

She looked in delight at their two blank faces.

Jago and Amica were stumped.

'I can't believe you don't know!' she said again, looking like she might burst with glee.

Jago was starting to find her inconclusiveness wearing.

'No, we don't know,' he said.

'What happened?' Amica urged, feeling the same.

The stranger beamed back at them, all her shyness apparently now gone. It was as if a different person stood before them.

'Well, we left, we all just got up and left!' she cried, 'The whole city, everyone's gone!'

'The whole city *left*?' said Jago in dismay.

'Yes!'

There was a stunned silence.

'How?' asked Amica finally.

'I don't really know exactly... The story goes...a few people just started leaving their units, they'd just had enough, I suppose. Then as soon as they realised nothing was actually happening outside...well,' she smiled, 'they started buzzing and banging on every door they could find. And so more joined them. Then *they* realised too: no fighting, no traitors, no danger at all. Then more left...then more, and soon the streets were full of people...

'I'm not sure quite how...I guess they'd just been pushed too far. I think for a long time, people had started to open their eyes, see the city for all its lies. So it wouldn't take much at that point, some small bit of impetus would do it. Maybe it was...the end of the families program or maybe...there was some rumour back; some bust up where civis made it out, I don't know...but something, something just made everyone snap.'

'So...then...people just walked right out of the city?' asked Jago.

'And the safeties didn't stop you?' Amica added.

'Yes. Well, we were walking around for a while, the group I was with anyway, we were just going wherever we wanted. But then, yes, most people just decided to leave altogether, they couldn't stomach being in the city any more. And as soon as people realised there was no perimeter, news spread. So yes, yes, people just abandoned the city, headed for the outside,' she paused for breath, '...*the safeties stop us*? Well they tried at first, of course, but, there were far too many of us. There were hundreds of us for every one of them probably, at least.'

She reflected for a moment, seeming to collate some thoughts.

Jago and Amica waited.

'You know, you can't keep it up forever,' she said, 'You can't lie and manipulate everyone all at once and for as long as you want. The so few can't keep controlling the so many, eventually the so many won't stand for it. We all have a breaking point, and the people had reached theirs.'

The significance of her story was beginning to set in for Amica and Jago. Had the city, the source of such agony for them, really just righted itself?

'So, what's going on there now?' said Amica.

'Not really sure,' replied the stranger, 'I heard when the guards realised there was not much they could do, they just lost interest. They sort of…became dispossessed, like they'd been deactivated or something. A lot took off their uniforms, some even left the city with the others. Can you imagine, a guard going against its programming?'

'Well, they're people too, of course,' Amica jumped in, '…underneath.'

'Right, sure. Anyway, so I guess the city is mostly empty, just some stragglers and some guards still knocking about. I mean, why would anybody stay there, when you've got all this?' She opened her arms out to show off the surroundings.

'Right, but why here? Why did you come *here*,' Jago enquired, it occurring to him, 'We're quite hard to find. Are you lost or something?'

'*Lost*?' she objected, 'No, I'm not lost. I grew up here, and now I'm back.' She grinned at them. 'I'm found, you might say.'

At this, the mood lightened as Jago and Amica were coming to terms with her story and beginning to trust her. If she was telling the truth, these were *her* old stomping grounds, much more so than theirs.

Jago looked at Amica for some confirmation.

Amica knew the city would hardly send someone out this far, certainly not someone alone. And she knew what fabrication looked like. Besides, she was tired of suspicion. She wanted to believe her.

She nodded at Jago. He nodded back.

'Okay, well, let's head to the village then,' Jago suggested, inducting the newcomer in.

'Yes, welcome back then, I suppose,' added Amica, 'What do we call you then, stranger?'

She smiled at them again.

'You can call me Pallas,' she said, 'What about you?'

7
BY THE FIRE

The day had passed, the sky benighted, a fire burnt below. Jago, Amica, Cato and Djuna were gathered around the fireplace. The usually boisterous kids had been tamed, albeit temporarily, by the prancing shapes and colours of the flames.

The four of them sat in silence.

'Dad?' Cato said, eventually brokering a conversation, 'You know the city...?'

'Yes...' Jago answered with foreboding.

'I don't understand,' said Cato.

Jago looked at him, 'What don't you understand, Cato?' he asked.

'Well...you were safe in the city, right?' he said.

'Depends from what,' Jago replied.

'Right, but no one got hurt...?'

'No, not if they stayed inside.'

'And no one got ill?'

'Not communicable deceases, no.'

'And no one ever died?'

'Generally not prematurely, no.'

'And you didn't ever have to work?'

'Most didn't, correct.'

'And everything was free?'

'In a way, yes.'

There was a long pause.

'So why was it so bad?' Cato said inquisitively, 'Wasn't everyone safe? Weren't you much safer than we are right now? I mean, it's more dangerous *out here*, isn't it?'

Jago sighed as he thought about it. Unwelcome memories of the city came back to him, his heart dropped at the mere thought of them, he would never be rid of them entirely. Cato had only ever had what he had now and would never know the city like he did.

He turned to his son, having formulated roughly his rejoinder.

'Cato, remember when you swam in the river yesterday, yes?' he said.

'Yes,' Cato replied.

'What if I told you you weren't allowed to do that any more?'

Cato frowned as he considered this.

'Why not?' he questioned.

'Well, because it's not safe to swim in rivers, Cato.'

'Isn't it?'

'No.'

'Oh.'

Cato looked puzzled.

'But it was safe to swim there yesterday...,' he noted.

'Yes, but now I've just decided it's not,' said Jago.

'...But it's the same river.'

'Right, but I've just decided it's not safe. Now, for your own good, you're never allowed to swim in that river ever again,' Jago continued, 'In fact, you're not allowed to swim in any river. No one is, never again, for ever and ever. Do you understand?'

Cato became visibly upset.

'But...I always swim in the river. You're saying I can't swim in any river ever again?' he said.

'That's correct, yes. You can't. It's not safe.'

'But...but shouldn't I be able to decide that for myself?'

'No, of course not, what a silly thing to say! I told you it's not safe and that is all you need to know.'

Cato trembled for a moment, on the verge of tears. Then he jumped up, and the flames of the fire reflected in his eyes and coloured his face red.

'But who are you to tell me what I can and cannot do?'

Jago then sat up imposingly and stared at him.

'Because...because... I am the king of the countryside,' he said, 'and I have decided that no one is ever allowed to swim in rivers ever again,' then he leant back, adding, 'Except me, of course.'

'What?' Cato exclaimed, '*You're* allowed to swim in the river?'

'Yes, of course, why wouldn't I be? I'm the countryside king.'

'But *I* want to swim in the river too.'

'I don't care about what you want,' Jago sat up sharply again, 'It's in the best interests of everyone that no one swims in rivers again, understand…? …Besides me, of course,' he added.

'But then…' Cato shook his head, '…then I don't have any choice.'

'No, you don't,' Jago said plainly.

There was a pause. The fire swelled.

'But I *should* have a choice,' Cato argued.

'Why should you?' Jago snapped, straightening up, 'What do *you* matter? You're just one person. Your wants do not matter, your opinion does not count. There is no choice, Cato, there is only what is in the best interest of the group. And you, young man, will do what you are told. And you will not swim in any river ever again, because I said so. And you have to do what I tell you.'

'No I don't! Not if it's not right.'

'Yes, you do. Because it's for your own good, and for the good of everybody. You don't get a say. You don't get a choice!'

The fire flared up.

'Yes, I do! And yes, I will!' Cato shouted emphatically, 'I *will* swim in the river. I will swim in the river every day, every day until I die. And I'll laugh at you standing on the bank whilst I'm doing it. Because I do have a choice. I am a person. And I *do* have a choice.'

His words rang out.

Jago had gotten the reaction he'd wanted and a species of pride overcame him nearly to tears. He saw in Cato someone who had argued against what he knew to be unfair and unjust, and who'd fought their corner even when barracked. He had surely now become a person of determination when tested and of strength when defending what he thought was right and moral.

'Yes, yes you do,' said Jago, as he hugged his child, hoping he might understand the lesson one day.

A little while later, when only the dregs of the fire smouldered and occasionally spat, the two children were fast asleep and Amica and Jago had sat serenely late into the evening.

'It's Pallas's birthday coming up,' Amica said, gently interrupting the quiet, 'She wants to see the moors again, after all this time.'

'Oh okay,' responded Jago, 'I think Bodhi said something about that too.'

Amica nodded. 'Yes. He's been so much better since she arrived, hasn't he; she's just what he needed. He's been on his own for all this time and it's so obvious he never really got over Draven. He's done nothing since that day, and depression makes homes of idle minds.'

'True,' Jago concurred.

The fire was depleting and they felt the first chill of the night. The children still looked content asleep in their blankets.

Jago and Amica embraced, wanting to keep warm and stay out for just a little while longer.

'You remember that night on the farm?' said Amica.

'Of course,' Jago replied.

Amica picked up some stones, then tilted her hand until they'd all rained down onto the ground.

A long pause ensued, pregnant with profundity for the both of them.

'To think if we hadn't met,' said Amica, 'you would've only just left the city with the rest of them, and I'd be...probably still wandering around in uniform...'

'It's hard to imagine. I don't want to.'

Jago held Amica closer.

They watched as the fire slowly went out and even the embers had dissolved into the dirt. They felt colder and shivered a little, but neither wanted to let go of the other.

END

Printed in Great Britain
by Amazon